Unrequited

Truth Devour

Published in 2013
by Truth Devour

Interior layout and design
by Publicious Pty Ltd
www.publicious.com.au

Book cover design by:
Brightpixel Design
www.brightpixeldesign.com.au

Catalogue-in-Publication details available
from the National Library of Australia

ISBN: 978-0-9922999-2-7

Also available in ebook
ebook ISBN: 978-0-9922999-3-4

To the man who resides between a spark and the flame. It was your fearless desire to reach my heart and dance with my soul that woke me from my emotional slumber. I spent most of my life believing you couldn't exist. I'II spend the rest of my days loving the fact that you do.

Unto my last breath it will be your name whispered to the universe as thanks.

Forever Grateful - Forever Loved - Always - Truth

ALSO BY TRUTH DEVOUR

Wantin
(1st book in the series)

Connected

I can hear the echoes of her laughter in a whisper. There is something familiar about her energy that binds me to her, forever present in a form that is not tangible or visible to my eye, yet she exists. I don't know her name or anything about her other than she is familiar to me. I can't recall the precise moment that she came into my life or a day without her being present. I love her as my own and have never questioned why.

The room was saturated with the smell of burning incense. The strategically placed esoteric images on the wall created an air of mystery. I was in a seat next to a stuffed raven, who stared at me. I felt as though it knew secrets I was yet to discover. I shifted in my seat to find a comfortable position as the clairvoyant walked into the room. This was my first time in the presence of a reader. I wasn't sure why I wanted to be here. I just knew that I had to listen to the messages channeled through her.

"Hello, my name is Lucinda." She smiled as her eyes looked me over.

I knew she was assessing my body positioning, so I

remained still with my arms open to demonstrate I was willing to allow her to read me.

"Hello, I'm Talia."

Lucinda smiled and shuffled the cards, all the while maintaining eye contact. I continued to sit as still as possible and returned her gaze. She was not aesthetically pretty but she resonated a beauty that felt welcoming.

"Do you come here seeking answers to questions?"

My hands moved to clasp one another in my lap. "No. I would like to hear what there is to be said with no direction placed."

She looked at my hands and smiled. I recognised the nervous tension rising in me. I had no idea why I was placing value in this experience. It was as though my subconscious was saying – finally you will hear me. It was a little unnerving to place such value on an external influence. I had been my own guide for the longest time.

"Clear your mind. Shuffle the cards and when you are ready split them in three sections with your left hand and then place them in a single pile in front of me."

I reached across for the cards and did what she asked. I closed my eyes, calmed my breath as I clumsily shuffled the deck. They felt soft in my hands, worn from frequent use. I found myself chanting the words 'show me what I need to see' in my mind as a mantra. An electric pulse caused me to stop the shuffle. In a trance, I broke the pack into three and then placed them back as one. Lucinda spread the deck and asked me to select twelve cards. She counted as I chose them.

"You are a very spiritual person, Talia. You already know the answers to the questions you choose not to ask."

I looked at her and didn't respond but whispered in my mind, *I know.*

One by one Lucinda carefully placed the cards in a specific order. I looked intently at the images. I had not played with tarot but felt I was able to read the messages that were presented before me. I took a deep breath, clasped my hands tight to reassure myself before placing them at my sides once more to remain open to receive what I already knew but didn't want to accept.

Lucinda looked at me in a quizzical manner as she conveyed the message. "The man you are with has death clouded above and below him. You know you have contributed to the sustainment of his life. He has cheated death because of your union."

"Yes," I said in a whisper, wanting to clasp my hands once more.

"All that you have given of yourself is returned in favour by his choice to deceive. Are you aware of his infidelity?"

"Yes."

"Still you hold steadfast to ensuring that he is safe from the reaper's grasp. Why?"

"I don't know why. I can only say that I want to. I continue to honour my desire to place him out of harm's way. My kindness exists without need for the return of such considerations."

Lucinda stared at me for the longest time before looking at the cards again.

"There is an end in what you offer to this man. It draws near. You will walk away but he will never let you go. You are unforgettable to him. Despite his behaviour, he loves you with a depth that is unbreakable. He binds himself you, but you do not bind yourself to him."

I was impressed by her ability to accurately depict the realities of my state without clouding it with her own judgement. I smiled with pursed lips and nodded. It was true. I hadn't allowed myself to fall in love with him. I loved him and did what was needed to be done to assist him for reasons unknown.

"There are many suitors here. You're not interested in them as they are in you. The path you choose is absent of companionship. You will take them as lovers at your leisure but none exist past the time you offer."

It was uncanny hearing a stranger speak my thoughts out loud. I knew my time with Sebastian would be drawing to a close and had decided I would never take another in my arms unless he was the one. I would rather live a lifetime with me than share a lifetime with the wrong person.

"You are protected by esoteric means. Do you dabble in witchcraft or elements of black magic?"

"No."

"There are powerful elements of voodoo that surround you. A woman placed this on you long ago to protect you. Do you know who this is?"

"Yes."

"She loves you still. You are always in her thoughts."

The clairvoyant had picked up on my connection to Marlee, my nanny when I was a child living in Haiti for a short stint. Marlee was present in my life at a time that was filled with my most tragic of losses. I knew I was well loved by her and was always grateful for it.

"You have been hiding from the world and yet it seeks you out. Your resistance is futile. You must allow yourself to emerge and trust what you have to offer will influence and benefit all that cross your path. Nothing you attempt ever fails. Use this ability to make a difference to more than just the one you help now."

I had been in hiding. I struggled with my ability to affect so many by just being present. I often felt overwhelmed by their response to me. I wanted people to feed the hunger they had by nourishing themselves rather than clamouring for what I might offer. It was one of my greatest struggles. I couldn't see what they saw in me.

"There is a man. He is your other. He searches for you. Do you know who this is?"

"No."

"You have crossed paths before. There is a karmic draw that pulls you together. Are you sure you don't know who this is?"

"If we've met before, I can't recall. I'm not sure who he is."

"He knows you. When the time is right, you will meet again. Did you know you have a little girl around you?"

I laughed. "Yes."

"Do you know who she is?"

"No, not really. Her essence has been around me for as long as I can remember. She's become my one constant. Always present through my darkest and happiest of times. I don't know why she's chosen me but I assume she's connected."

"Yes. She has chosen you. She's your unborn daughter."

I heard myself swallow and my heartbeat increased as I shook my head. "No, I have no intention of bringing a life into this world. She's wasting her time if that's what she seeks."

"She was clapping her hands and dancing around you when I spoke about this man. Perhaps she knows something that you do not."

I turned to face a space to my right, where I knew she was standing. "I'm sorry, little one. I won't do it. In this lifetime I will never have a child. Please find another."

Lucinda took a deep breath and allowed herself to release her tears. "Do you know what she is doing now?"

"She's cuddling me and holding my hand," I said in a choked-up voice.

"She loves you and won't ever leave you."

The tears started to well in the corner of my eyes. I felt relieved that the essence of this little girl was determined to stay, mixed with a sadness that she might waste her opportunity to be born through another while waiting for me.

"You have an amazing gift, Lucinda."

"Not unlike your own, Talia. Nothing that we spoke of today was unknown to you. Why did you seek clairvoyance when you were already in the space of knowing?"

"When you live a life of seeing what's to occur ahead, there are times when I wonder if I'm missing something because I've relied on all that I see. This experience gives me the opportunity to find out if there are any blind spots in my knowing."

She laughed. "Have you found your blind spot?"

"Yes, I believe I have."

"Would you do me the honour of sharing this with me, as I don't see it?"

"I want a person whose vibration matches the tune my soul sings. My desire is to have our hearts synchronised as one. I believed in this lifetime it would never exist for me. A gypsy in the forests of Hungary once told me a man seeks me. The cards have told me again today this is still true. Yet I cannot see him or when he arrives. I am blinded to his moves."

Lucinda smiled. "Ah, I feel that fate is playing you a kindness here."

"How?"

"A person who has the gift of seeing all is left with little surprise. You are not meant to see him coming and will not be able to resist him when he arrives." She sat back and folded her arms and smiled with satisfaction.

I returned her smile as I reflected. I couldn't recall the last time I was surprised nor imagine anyone approaching me without me knowing.

I rose to my feet and said thanks.

She enfolded me in a warm embrace and told me I was welcome. I walked out of that experience feeling a renewed delight in the possibility of the unknown. I looked forward to the future but knew I had matters that needed to be addressed in the present.

It was time.

Forever

Sebastian was sitting in the lounge room playing his guitar. As always, his face lit up when I walked into the room. I knew I would miss that most about him.

"How was your day, honey bun?" he asked in an unusually chirpy voice.

I stood in the doorway and looked at him. I wanted to drink in the last moments that we would have together.

"What's up, hon?"

"I was just thinking about our last five years together."

"It's been five and a half and still counting," he said, still very melodically.

I moved across to sit in the armchair. I reclined it and positioned myself to face him.

He pouted as he moved his guitar to one side. "Where's my kiss?"

I looked at my hands and shrugged my shoulders. "I went and saw a clairvoyant today."

He shifted to be closer to me and nervously asked, "What did they say?"

"She said you're cheating on me." I looked at him and saw the expression on his face alter to fear.

"That's ridiculous. I would never do that to you. I love you." The pitch in his voice had changed to be higher than normal. He reached out to touch my arm.

I stared at his hand squeezing my arm and sighed. In a calm voice, I said, "Don't do this. Don't lie to me. The only thing I ever asked for was your honesty, nothing more. Please. Tell me the truth."

"Talia, honestly – whatever she said was wrong. Why would you believe her and not me?" His tone indicated his annoyance.

"She didn't tell me anything I didn't already know: She's a brunette, approximately five-foot-six, slender build. You met her at the party I didn't go to last week. She kissed you and you never stopped her. She offered you an opportunity for more and you took it. The thing is you had already met her somewhere else, online or in a coffee house. This wasn't an accident; it was premeditated."

Sebastian raised an eyebrow, "You got all this from a clairvoyant?"

I shook my head, astounded at his question. "No, that part was what I already knew because I saw it before it happened. The clairvoyant confirmed your betrayal through the reading, nothing more."

"Hang on. If you knew I was apparently going to do something, why didn't you stop me?"

"I believe in free will. It's your life and therefore your choice. Who am I to interfere with your chosen path?"

His voice changed to anger. "So what you're telling me is you thought I was going to have an affair. You didn't stop me in this hypothetical endeavour and now some crazy pagan tells you that I've slept with someone and you believe them."

"No, Seb; I believe me."

He raised his voiced louder as he stood up. "I didn't sleep with ANYONE."

I felt an overwhelming sadness. After all we had been through, he was unable to offer me the only thing I needed from him: the truth. I slowly stood up and walked towards the front door.

He followed me down the narrow corridor. "Where are you going?" he said with concern.

I placed my hand on the door and leaned my head on my arm. "I'm afraid that's no longer any of your business. I'll be back later. Maybe then you'll be willing to tell me the truth."

I walked out the door and jumped in my car. He stood in the doorway, speechless, watching me drive down the road. I had no idea where to go. I didn't want to be among strangers and had no desire to speak about this with friends. I needed some time to think things through.

I found myself sitting at the local botanical gardens, staring into the manmade lake with emptiness in my heart. All I wanted was the truth. I had lived with him through his darkest times. I had reached beyond the threshold of death to bring him back and yet he was still unable to offer me the only thing that ever mattered. The strangest part was I didn't care that he had slept with someone else.

***

I arrived home and there he was sitting on our bed with his head in his hands.

"Hey," was all I could think of to say. My gut was wrenched with sorrow. Watching him in turmoil gave me no pleasure.

His hands were still covering his face when he said, "I did cheat."

"OK," was my response to the very thing I had already known.

I walked into the kitchen and put the kettle on then I sat at the table waiting for the kettle to boil. Once I'd made myself a cup of green tea, I drank it slowly. *What to do next?* I had no desire to yell, get angry or to cry. I was disappointed and partly relieved.

"Talia."

I looked at Sebastian, who was now standing next to me. His eyes were swollen and red from crying. I could see he was in a world of hurt and knew there was nothing I could ever do to ease his pain. This was his to own and process in any way he chose.

"I'm really sorry. It was a onetime thing; it won't happen again," he said, believing his own babble.

"Sure it will." I took another sip of my tea.

"It won't. I never wanted to hurt you."

"I'm not sure if you believe what you're saying or saying it because you feel it's the right thing. The truth is you were chirpy and happy about your indiscretion until you got confronted. Try and be honest at least with yourself, even if you're not able to be with me."

I could see my words were finally starting to seep past his default thinking.

"I guess you're going to break up with me then."

"No, Seb. I won't break up with you. If you want to leave, you need to break up with me."

Deep crinkles appeared on his brow as he raised his eyebrows and narrowed his eyes. "You said cheating was a deal-breaker."

Casually shrugging my shoulders, I responded, "I did say it, but now, living in the moment, I've changed my mind. You're forgiven."

"Why? You always said you'd leave me if I did something like this."

"It's funny. If I didn't know any better, I would say you seem angry I'm choosing to forgive you. I thought you would be happy. I'm sure we could work through this."

"You're doing this on purpose. You know I could never leave you. I could never be the one to leave you." Sebastian burst into tears. His body heaved as he gasped for air.

I watched quietly as he worked himself into an emotional frenzy. He was determined not to be the instigator of the very thing that he desired.

Over and over he blurted the words, "I can't leave you."

I waited patiently for him to compose himself. I wanted him to at least be man enough to break up with me. I thought that was the least that he could do, given the circumstances.

***

Two hours into his continued crying, I had to succumb. It was clear now it would never happen unless I did it. I was exhausted watching him in emotional turmoil. My instinct to comfort and protect were greater than my desire for him to do something he clearly wasn't capable of.

I placed my arms around him and held him as he sobbed into my neck. I stroked his hair and rocked him as I would to comfort a child. I had taken it too far. He was beyond consoling. This had never been my intention.

"It's OK, Seb. I'm breaking up with you. It's OK. Shhhhh."

His arms squeezed me tightly as he howled. The pain surging through him struck a chord with me and made me feel like a heel. I knew he loved me because of the journey we had taken together; a path that no one else would ever understand. I was the keeper of his secrets, the protector, the nurturer and his best friend. He was torn between the ideals of loving me versus his desire to be single.

"It's OK. You'll be OK. I'll help you get through this. Shhhhh." I continued to console him.

Hours passed with Seb buried deep in my arms. He lay quietly breathing shallow breaths. I couldn't think past the moment. This was it for us. This was to be our forever. I couldn't help wondering: if he had died during our time together, would he have been considered my best love? Would I have spent my remaining days in a delusion that he had been my ideal? It was amazing to think, after all we had been through during his illness, it had ended like this for us.

***

In the morning, I helped him pack some things so he could leave to stay at a friend's. I needed to reclaim my space and he needed to process what had happened and what he wanted to do next with his newly obtained freedom. I knew as I watched him drive away all was as it should be. He was heading down a new pathway and I was free to re-establish mine. I could finally breathe again.

***

The first week was the hardest in my transition to being single. I missed receiving his calls and having his warmth beside me at night. It's only ever in the absence of someone that you can really identify the smaller things

13

which you might have taken for granted. He used to leave for work earlier than I did so he would leave secret notes in places where I would find them. I would fall asleep listening to him playing his guitar. I missed that he would follow me everywhere I went in the house and settle down near me so he could be close. It used to drive me nuts and now I kind of missed it. The first time I heard the song *My Immortal* by Evanescence I recognised what I was feeling. It was a rude awakening to realise, with him gone, I had to re-establish who I was to me. I had lost myself in the demands of the relationship. This was something I would never allow again.

***

Sebastian came by the house a couple of weeks later to gather his things. Originally, I wasn't going to be there, but then decided at the last minute that I should stay. When he arrived, he was surprised to see me.

"Hey," he said as he walked in the door.

"G'day."

"Sorry, I wasn't expecting you to be here. Do you want me to go?"

"Nope – I'm all good. I've packed most of your things in these boxes. The rest was too big."

"Wow. OK. Thanks."

"No problems."

He placed his hands in his jeans' pockets. "How are you?"

"Good, thanks for asking. How are you?"

Sebastian's face contorted slightly. "I miss you." He paused. "I miss us."

I nodded. "It will pass. I'll help you load the car."

He looked at me while I walked across, picked up one of the boxes and brushed past him to reach the door.

Once outside, I placed the box near the car and returned to fetch another.

"Can we talk?" he asked in a sad tone.

I knew nothing good was going to come from holding this discussion. I wanted the closure to be swift and simple and he was holding steadfast in his desire to elongate the process.

I released a long exhale. "OK, what would you like to talk about?"

"Can we go into the lounge? I want to sit and talk with you for a bit before we say our final goodbyes. I need to do this."

It took a conscious effort not to roll my eyes and show my contempt for his request. Instead I walked into the lounge and sat on the recliner. He looked at my choice of seat and shook his head as he sat as close as he could on the couch beside me.

"I loved you. I need you to know that. I've always loved you. That's never changed for me. You are always going to be loved by me. You saved my life. I'm never going to be able to repay that debt and I'm always going to regret the way things ended between us."

I maintained my gaze on my hands. "OK."

"Is there anything you want me to tell you?"

"Nope, I'm good."

"Aren't you even curious about why I did this?"

"It's OK; I already know."

"How?"

Raising my head, I looked directly into his eyes. "Seb, it's obvious. Let's just leave it. I'm OK. I'd prefer to skip this part and get back to loading up the car."

"No, Talia. Tell me what you think the reason is. I don't want to leave here wondering if you really know what drove me to this. It's important to me. Please."

I took a deep breath, shook my head and explained. "You were born with an illness that haunted your early years. I was the first girlfriend you ever had. I was the only one you had ever slept with. All your life people saw you as a sick person. Your illness provided a cloak which defined your core being. I came along and saw past this; I saw you. When you were blessed with the cure you needed, things changed. People now saw beyond the mask of the illness and met you. They gave you attention, flirted, and you enjoyed it. Seb, you spent your whole life fighting to live. I get that you now want to explore possibilities, and being with other people is a large part of it. The last thing I would want is for you to stay with me out of some false obligation and then upon your deathbed look at me with eyes of regret. I always knew our journey would end when you received the cure you required. I just hoped for a better ending. That's all."

"It's taken me weeks to figure this out. How the hell did you know?"

"I just do. Things appear to be clear when you're committed to telling and seeing the truth no matter what the cost."

He reached out to touch my arm and I recoiled. He paused for a moment. "You never cease to amaze me."

"Are we done?"

Seb shook his head and blurted out, "I'm dating Lucy."

"I know."

"She understands my need to experiment and said she's OK with me sleeping with other people. So … if you ever wanted to … you know."

"Seb, it was never about the sex. If it was then I would have left you a long time ago."

"Cheez, Talia, take it easy. I wasn't that bad."

"I'm not trying to be cruel, just honest. You were sick for a long time. The sex was compromised and not as good as you imagined it in your head, so, no, I'm not really up for a little bit on the side from my ex. Thanks for asking." I winked and patted him on the knee as I stood up. "Are we done with this conversation now?"

Sebastian played with his hands. "I want to still be in your life. I don't want to imagine a world without you in it."

I looked at him. I knew he thought his words were sincere but now I was starting to feel annoyed. I had given him all of me in the time we spent together and he chose to end things in a disrespectful way and yet he still wanted more.

I folded my arms. "What would you offer me in this friendship?"

I saw the blood drain from his face as he continued to stare at his hands. "I know I haven't been the best boyfriend but I want to make it up to you in friendship."

"I understand the intent. What I would like to know is exactly what you would offer me in friendship?"

"I don't know what you want me to say?"

"Do you offer me trust, loyalty, reliability, respect?"

"I'm going to try."

"Do you offer me friendship because you feel you still need me? Are you scared something will happen and I won't be there to catch you?"

"No."

I raised an eyebrow. "Really? Are you sure?"

"I know you have more to offer me than I will ever be able to offer you. It doesn't change the fact that I want you in my life. No one is ever going to understand what we went through over those years. No one."

"Not true. I will never forget and neither will you. It doesn't provide a reason to remain in touch. You need to walk your path and I want to be left alone. I gave you all I have to offer and it still wasn't enough for you to give me the only thing I wanted: honesty."

"I'm never going to give up on you."

"Let's pack the rest of these boxes into your car so you can head off." I walked out of the room and carried more of the boxes to his vehicle.

I had reached my limit of being nice. I was annoyed with his lecherous need to stay in my life. I had no more to offer him. He had received more from me than I had ever provided to another and yet he hungered for more. When he had packed the last of his things he turned to walk back towards the house to say goodbye. I placed my hand up to halt him and with sadness in my heart attempted a half-smile before closing the door. I didn't want him to touch me.

I was done.

In Search of Self

I had always been thankful for my natural ability to disconnect from anything that no longer served me. My journey with Sebastian had been an important part of my growth as a woman. He was present in my life at a time when I needed to feel what it meant to be loved. His illness provided a state of mind that promoted the importance of today because there was never a guarantee of tomorrow. At the time we met it was a very attractive attribute to me. I knew I could never deny the love I had held for him but I also recognised it had taken its course. I was never in love with him, I never wanted to marry him and I had no desire to have his children.

I was exhausted. I had no more to offer him or any other. I no longer saw a point in being in a relationship unless I was presented with the right one. Moving forward, I would walk alone into a future of my creation. This was the first time in years that I felt free.

All my bags were packed. The house we had rented together held too much history. I no longer wanted to be bound to a person let alone a place. Most of my personal effects were now in storage. The few possessions

I planned to take with me were already in the trunk of my car. It was time to hit the road.

I arrived at Ruth and Shane's house in record time. My aunty's face lit up when she saw me. It had been nearly two years since I was last at the homestead. Nothing had changed; time did not punish her beauty.

"Talia, sweetheart. Oh, how I have missed that smile," she said as she put her hands on my face.

"Hello."

"Come in. We just set the table for dinner."

I grabbed my bags and followed her in.

"Talia," called out Shane as he came towards me and gave me a big grizzly bear hug. "You are a sight for sore eyes."

I laughed. "Hey, Shane, good to see you too."

The rest of the family formed an orderly queue to cuddle me. Suzanna, Tommy, Sammy; all held me in the warmth of their embrace. The nieces and nephews impatiently clamoured for their turn. My favourite little girl, Mia, was now seven and a half years old. She had Brad's eyes and the cheekiest smile.

Brad stood back patiently waiting until I finished acknowledging all the kids. I looked at him smirking at me and shook my head, laughing.

"Come here," I said with my arms wide open.

He walked across and put his arms around me and squeezed my breath out as he lifted my body and swung me in a circle.

"Welcome home," he whispered as he inhaled the scent from my hair.

I was seated at the head of the table. Ruth and Suzanna brought out all the food while the rest of us tried to settle the kids into their seats. This place held so many memories for me. Now the next generation was obtaining memories of their own. It was truly nice to be here.

"Where's Sebastian?"

"He's in Melbourne catching up with some friends," I said as I reached for my glass of wine.

I didn't tell them what had happened. It was still too fresh in my mind to talk about and I didn't want them to worry. Ruth had always been concerned that I would never settle down. The last thing I needed was for them to spend the rest of my visit consumed with something I had come here to forget.

"Tell me, what's new?" I said to divert any further discussion about Seb.

"The old horse riding school is up for sale," said Brad with a twinkle in his eye.

"Really? I thought they were never going to sell that place."

"The owners want to retire and have decided to move to a residential in town. It's not on the market yet but the real estate agent told me it's going on the market next week," said Brad.

He knew I had always loved the property.

"I know what a period is," yelled Mia to draw attention to her.

"Really, Mia? Can you explain it to me?" I smiled wickedly at the silence at the table.

"Talia, no," said Suzanna, horrified by what Mia might say.

"No, I'm interested to know what a period is. Can you please tell me, Mia?" I said, absolutely delighted by the angst Mia had created in the room.

"It's a full stop," she said, beaming with pride.

I laughed as I felt the sigh of relief from everyone.

"Ah, yes. You are indeed correct, young lady, and very clever." I looked across at Suzanna. "It is a full stop. I think we should all make a toast to periods."

"Oh, Talia," said Ruth, laughing.

She raised her glass, as did the others, saluting the idea of periods. Mia beamed from ear to ear.

"So, are you interested in inspecting the riding school? We could have a look at it tomorrow," said Brad, persisting in his need to bait me.

I took another sip of my wine. "Maybe."

"Oh, Talia, it would be wonderful to have you living up the road from all of us," said Ruth, clapping her hands in approval.

Brad smirked and kicked me under the table. I smiled and shook my head again. He had an amazing way of managing me that I enjoyed. He was the only one in my life I felt a profound connection to.

***

Post dinner we all gathered in the lounge room to play charades. It was nice to be in a space filled with laughter. Ruth and Shane had three beautiful children and were blessed with five wonderful grandchildren. Tommy had married Lisa, his high school sweetheart, and Sammy had married James, a gentle man of tall stature. I envied the simplicity of their lives. I was always so restless in comparison.

After a while, Ruth said to the kids, "It's time for bed."

"No, we want a bedtime story," yelled Mia as the others nodded their heads and jumped around to solidify their message of approval.

"Aunty Talia, can you read us a story?" asked Mia as she crawled into my lap.

"Sure, one story and then off to bed. OK?" I said, holding up a finger.

"Yeah," they all screamed.

"What would you like me to read?" I asked.

Mia ran out the room and returned just as quickly with a Dr Suess book called *Horton Hears a Who*. All the kids gathered around as I read them the story. Ruth, Suzanna, Sammy and Lisa went into the kitchen to do the supper dishes while Tommy, James and Shane went outside to sit on the porch to smoke cigars. Only Brad remained in the room, watching in the background. It amused him to see me immerse myself in a children's book to entertain the troops.

When the kids were asleep, the rest of the clan headed off to bed, knowing the demands of their offspring would start again at the break of dawn. I was a night owl and rarely slept for longer than a few hours at a time. I finished the last of my wine and went outside to sit on the porch. The air was still, the stars were out in splendour and the scent of the eucalypts was present. I was one month away from turning thirty and I had no idea what I planned to do next with my life.

I smiled as I heard the creak of the floorboards and the door squeak open as he approached. I didn't need to turn around; I knew it was Brad. I felt him watching me in the shadows.

As he sat beside me on the edge of the porch, he said, "Tell me what happened."

"With what?" I knew exactly what he was referring to.

"Did he hurt you?" He had an expression of concern on his face.

"No, don't be silly. Nothing happened; it's all good." I placed my hand on his knee and squeezed it.

"Talia, don't lie. You can fool them but never me. I know you're not telling me the whole truth. Talk to me." He placed his hand on mine and intertwined his fingers.

"I'd forgotten how beautiful this place is," I said, staring up at the night sky.

"Try again," he responded impatiently.

I looked at him and smiled as I took a deep breath. Brad was such a beautiful soul. How on earth was I supposed to explain what had happened?

"Talia, come on. You're scaring me." He lifted my hand and kissed my palm.

"We broke up."

"Why?" He coaxed the conversation along.

"It was time, that's all. Let's talk about something else."

"Nope. Tell me why."

I was annoyed by his persistence. "Seriously?"

"Yes, seriously. You never share your pain. I want you to trust me. Tell me what's happening. I love you and I want to know. Please." He placed his arm under mine and clasped my hand once again. His grip was fierce.

I looked at our hands and shook my head. "You're impossible, Brad Parker."

He laughed. "I know. Now tell me."

"Seb was cheating on me. I confronted him and he chose to lie about it. He eventually conceded and told me the truth, or at least the version he was capable of telling, and we broke up. That's it; nothing more to tell." I shrugged my shoulders.

"That fucking prick! After everything you did for him. Are you serious? What a fucking arsehole! Why on earth would he of all people cheat on you? I don't get it." He shuffled in closer to me.

I could hear the anger in his voice.

"Don't do that. Don't be angry with him. It's OK. This is just the way it was meant to be," I said with sadness in my voice.

"Um, no. It's not OK; he's an arse. He had the woman of my dreams in his arms and he took you for granted. That's just shit, Talia."

Tension rose through my body. I didn't want to have to explain myself but I had no choice now. If I left it this way, Brad would carry the burden of anger. It wasn't required from him or from me.

"This is why I didn't want to talk about it. It's not a bad outcome. I'm OK and Seb is going to be OK too."

"Why are you protecting him? You're always playing the martyr; don't do that. He's a bastard for what he did to you. Damn right I'm fucking angry. You couldn't have been kinder and he's rewarded you with this. Are you fucking kidding me?" His voice was raised and he dropped my hand in disgust.

"Shhh, you'll wake the others."

"I'm never going to understand how you allow yourself to be a doormat."

I jumped off the porch and turned to face Brad. "No, no, no. Don't start, Brad. Come on, this is not what I need right now. A doormat? Do you mind?" I couldn't believe he had called me that. I folded my arms and stared at him. "Fuck. Seriously, come on."

"So you get pissed off at this, but you don't show any emotion about what that creep did to you?" he hissed.

"Just listen. When you went through puberty you were graced with the experiences of a normal teen: flirting with girls, losing your virginity, sexually exploring. Seb was the sick kid that the other kids teased and bullied. They threw stuff at him because he wasn't able to run.

None of the girls showed interest in him. He was denied the rite of passage we all take for granted in our teens."

"So that entitles him to fuck around behind your back?" he sniped.

"Shut up and listen. The reality is, when he received the cure, he started to feel better. He put on some weight and there was colour in his cheeks. His newfound health brought interest from other women. Given I was his first, he felt torn between the flirtatious advances that were being made and his commitment to me. I recognised he was going through some changes and offered to break up with him so he could sow his wild oats. He refused and held steadfast to the concept of 'us'. I knew it was more to do with him being scared. I was the only love he had known and, as enticing as these sirens were, he was not ready to take flight. So I waited. It only took a few months before I noticed the change in his behaviour. He stayed up late on the computer and snuck phone calls to people. I never gave him any indication that I was aware of what was happening. I chose to let it take its course. He eventually found the opportunity he was seeking, but sadly was not brave enough to be honest. I guess he thought he might be able to have his cake and eat it. I confronted him a week after the indiscretion occurred and he denied it. Eventually the truth came out and we broke up."

Brad shook his head while he played with his hands.

"It's OK, I promise." I placed my hand back on his knee.

The sincerity returned to his voice. "How can you be so forgiving?"

"I guess I don't see that there's anything to forgive. I didn't do anything wrong. It's Sebastian who will have to find a way to forgive himself for the way he chose to end things." I turned and looked at the sky and placed my arms out as if to embrace the universe.

Brad walked behind me; his hands glided along the length of my arms and he entwined his fingers in mine. He crossed my arms around my body and rested his head into the back of my neck. "You're amazing," he whispered.

I smiled and pushed my head back against his forehead. "Funny. I could have sworn I was a doormat a minute ago."

"Sorry."

"Don't mention it to the others. It's not a secret; I just don't have the energy to manage the rollercoaster of emotions they'd go through about this. I know Ruth will worry and there's honestly no need. I'm fine. OK?"

"OK," he said as he nuzzled deeper into the back of my neck. He inhaled my scent. "I've missed you so much."

I laughed as I worked my way out of his grasp to face him. "Time for bed, you."

He reached out, grabbed my hand and led me inside. He placed his hands on my face and said, "You will be his greatest loss."

I nodded, left him there and walked into my old bedroom, closing the door behind me.

***

I woke to the sound of a herd of elephants running through the house. Mia was calling my name. I squinted at the light beaming through my bedroom window. Releasing a groan, I placed a pillow over my head. I needed more sleep. Just as I was about to drift off again, the door opened.

"Rise and shine, sleepyhead," said Brad in a cheerful voice.

I put my arm in the air, waving. "Go away."

"Kids, it looks like Aunty Talia needs some help getting out of bed," yelled Brad.

In stormed the troops. Leaping onto me with no mercy, they screeched and giggled as they took my pillow and peeled away my doona to find my hands. Brad remained in the doorway, laughing heartily.

"OK, OK. I'm getting up," I said as I reached for the first child I could find and started to mercilessly tickle. "Right, who's next?" I yelled as I tossed Jack aside to make way for my next wriggling victim.

They all, much to my surprise, lined up to be tickled. It amused me to witness the purity of their joy. I needed to be here.

***

After breakfast, Brad and I headed out the door. Suzanna came with us and stood on the veranda to wave goodbye.

"We'll return soon," I said, waving back.

She laughed. "No, you won't."

I looked at Brad as he said, "Shh, it's a surprise."

Suspicious, I responded, "What's a surprise? What are you up to?"

"It's OK, Talia. Brad wants you all to himself. He's been planning this for weeks. Just make sure you're home in time to put the kids to bed." She walked back inside.

Brad had a deliciously wicked smile on his face. "Get in the car and no more questions."

I got in, buckled up and we headed down the road. The first stop was the riding school. As we approached the entrance, beautiful memories flooded my mind. It was exactly how I remembered it as a child. When the car was parked I made a beeline straight to the stables. Inside, I gazed at the craftsmanship; they didn't make buildings like this anymore. The predominant material used was wood supplied from the neighbouring plantation. The solid structure needed a little tender love and care but all in all was in good order. I felt disappointed the stables were empty. They used to be filled with a mish-mash of horses.

I pouted. "Where are all the horses?"

"They sold them a few weeks ago at an auction."

"Bugger, I was looking forward to seeing them."

"I have the keys to the house. Come on," he said as he walked out of the stable yard.

I followed, wondering why Brad had the keys to the house. Inside, the place was empty. I looked at Brad, who was not volunteering any information. Each of the rooms was spectacular in size. The light beamed through it, creating welcome warmth that resonated with a feeling of homeliness.

Brad finally broke the silence as we entered the last room. "Well, what do you think?"

"What do you think I think, Mr Know-it-all?" I said smugly.

He laughed as he leaned against the wall and gazed at me. He paused for a moment and then said, "Sold."

"Indeed." I released my breath.

His voice almost squealed, "Really, you mean it?"

"Yep, I really mean it. This place has to stay in the family."

He jumped in the air. "I knew it!"

"Someone's very happy with himself," I said, laughing at his excitement.

"Are you kidding? This means you'll be close by. Finally you've made a decision to lay down some foundations. It's awesome, Talia, and long overdue."

"Whatever. I'll have to call the agent and work out a deal." I was trying to keep my excitement contained.

Brad reached into his jacket and pulled out an envelope. "Actually, I already have the paperwork ready for you to sign."

"Are you serious? Were you so sure that I'd buy the place?"

He walked across to where I was standing. "Yep, here's a pen."

"I think I'll have my lawyer look over the paperwork first, if you don't mind," I said as I snatched the contract from him.

"It's all above board. It's a standard contract. I already had the family lawyer assess it for you. He did all the title checks. It's ready to sign."

I reached across, took the pen from his hand and blindly signed the contract. Given my inheritance, money was not an issue so the price they asked was fine by me. I wanted this place and was blessed with the luxury of being able to afford it.

"Wait right here," said Brad as he ran out the door.

In his absence, I took the time to give myself a hug, swinging from side to side. I'm home, I thought to myself. This is it for me.

Brad came in with a bottle of champagne and two flutes. I clapped as he popped the cork and poured.

"To new beginnings. Welcome home, Talia," he said in a syrup-like self-satisfied tone.

I clinked my glass against his. "To new beginnings."

"OK, drink up. We need to go. There's much to do today."

Before I could finish the last of my champagne, Brad dragged me out of the door. I could see he was having a blast. I knew resistance was futile, so I jumped back in the car and looked at the passing scenery as he drove me to our next destination.

He parked the car in town and took me to a furniture store. He winked as the sales lady came across and kissed him hello.

I could hear her whisper, "Did she buy it?"

Brad was beaming with pride as he said, "She sure did."

"Oh, that's wonderful. Congratulations." She peered over Brad's right shoulder.

"Thanks."

"Let me show you what we have on the showroom floor." She gestured for me to come closer.

I listened as she told me about the furniture. I could see she expected to have a good sales' day. I wanted nothing more than to make it happen for her but most of what I saw was very outdated. Brad didn't help things by pulling faces behind her back when she described each piece. This was fun. I was actually having a great time.

We resorted to looking through the catalogues that had more to offer than the stagnant style presented in the store. After an hour of trawling through the pages, I finally started to see some pieces that suited my eclectic taste. I placed my orders and we left to find some lunch.

Brad took me to Ming Chows, the finest Chinese restaurant in town. In truth, it was the only Chinese restaurant in town. Every rural district had one. We were the only ones dining in, so we had the pick of the tables. It was nice to have time out with Brad. It felt like old times, except we were older and presumably wiser.

"Have anything you like; my shout," he said, peering over the menu.

"In that case, I will have one of everything. I'm famished." I closed the menu and placed it in front of me.

"That's nice to hear for a change: you wanting to eat rather than me having to trick you into it."

I ignored his comment and placed my order with the waitress. She took Brad's order and scurried behind the curtains into the kitchen.

"So what's next in your bag of tricks?" I hoped he might succumb to revealing the rest of his plans.

"All in good time, Missy. Be patient. All will be revealed in good time."

"Why are you doing this?" I asked, looking into his eyes.

"Because I can," he said in a chirpy tone.

I paused for a moment, wondering whether I needed to really push the point or let it slide. Against my better judgment, I persisted. "Tell me why. I'd like to know."

His expression changed as he returned my gaze. Brad had amazing eyes that seemed to look right through me. "I owe you so much for everything you've done for me. I'm so happy in my life and I'm not sure that I would have had all I do if it wasn't for you. I put you through so much and against all odds you held steadfast and did what needed to be done despite the price paid. I'll never forget it. I need to give you something in return."

I thought about his words. My mind flitted back to the moments we had shared and the difficulties we had faced in the space we had created for one another. "You owe me nothing, Brad. Everything is as it should be. You possess what you have because you chose to embrace it. It has nothing to do with me. It was all you."

He reached across the table and placed his hand on mine. "You're the reason I learnt to love."

I picked up his hand and kissed it. "OK."

He smiled, knowing I wasn't going to accept his version of reality but was no longer going to attempt to convince him to align with my own. We each had differing views on our past; acceptance of this was the key to moving forward.

When the food arrived I poured a cup of tea for each of us and held my cup in the air to make a toast. "To imaginary debts now paid in full."

Brad lifted his cup. "Forever indebted; forever grateful; forever loved."

We sipped our tea and ate the food in silence. There is something to be said about not needing to fill the air with noise for the sake of it. Brad and I were as comfortable as a worn old pair of work boots. Moulded to fit one another perfectly.

The next stop was up a road I had never been on before. The track ended and we parked the car. I could see a narrow path leading into the bush land.

"Hiking?" I asked.

"Follow me. Make sure you keep up," he said with a smile.

We walked up the steady incline. The higher we got the wetter the terrain became. As we approached a clearing, I could hear water. It had me curious. Flashbacks of our childhood adventures danced in my mind as we reached the top of an open field. To our left was an amazing rock pool that was the resting place for the water tumbling from a cliff face above it.

"Ta-dah," he said with his arms spread out.

I walked across to the water's edge. "This is incredible. How did you find it?"

"I was looking for property in the area. I came to look at this property and bought it on the spot."

"Wow, this is yours and Suzanna's. That's fantastic. What a magic location."

"I know. I couldn't believe my luck."

Brad walked me around the flat of the land, pointing out the house site and explaining all his plans for development. I couldn't stop smiling. I was so happy for him. His life was charmed and with this property he had everything that he had ever dreamed of as a child.

Unexpectedly, he turned and grabbed my hand to lead me back to the water's edge. "There's someone I want you to meet."

I followed him and waited patiently as he scoured the perimeter of the water.

"He must be on the other side. Come on." He walked into the water fully clothed.

I knew he was determined to show me something. This was his day as much as it was mine, so in blind faith I walked into the cool waters. The pool was deeper than I expected and suddenly Brad was up to his shoulders. I laughed and started to retract, but he leaped forward and grabbed me so that I fell on him. Our heads dunked under and we both resurfaced, laughing. We swam across to the other side and once again Brad scanned the edge looking for something.

"Talia, here," he said in a whisper, pointing down.

I quietly positioned myself next to him and peered down.

"I've called him Barry Junior," he said as he placed his hand over mine and squeezed.

"Hello, Barry Junior," I whispered. Tears welled in my eyes.

I watched the little platypus foraging between the rocks for food, happily unaware we were standing over him. I was lost for words. Brad simply knew how to touch my heart unlike any other.

He turned and placed me in his arms. I wrapped mine around his torso and closed my eyes. Tears rolled down my cheeks. This was an unexpected delight.

"I love you, Talia. Don't ever forget that," he said, choked on his words.

"I love you, too, more than you will ever know. Thanks for this. It means the world to me."

Slowly, we made our way back across the rock pool and onto the other side to head to the car. Brad kept turning to check on me as we walked down the path in our wet shoes. When we reached the bottom, he cheekily lifted both my arms out and inspected me from head to toe.

"Pity there isn't a local wet T-shirt competition to enter you in," he said, laughing.

I reefed my hands down and folded my arms to hide my visible assets.

"Nicely planned, cheeky monkey."

In a confident tone, he responded, "That wasn't planned. It was more of a happy accident."

He winked as he opened the car door for me and pretended to attempt one last look. I punched him in the arm and pushed him away, laughing. He still had a definite charm about him.

***

By the time we arrived home, we were freezing. The car heater had been on but it wasn't strong enough to take the chill from our clothes. I rushed in the door to get first dibs on a hot shower.

As I opened the door, I was stunned by the family yelling, "Surprise!"

Ruth came forward when she saw I was dripping wet. "Talia, you're drenched."

Brad walked in behind me, soaked to the bone. "Don't blame me, Mum. Talia insisted on going for a swim and then I had to jump in to save her."

"Ha, ha. Yeah, that sounds realistic. Give your folks more credit than that, Brad," I said, sticking my tongue out at him.

"Let's get you out of these wet clothes. We can get the explanation later," said Ruth impatiently.

***

After my shower, I went into the lounge and was greeted with another group-shout. "Surprise!"

I looked up and saw a banner with 'Congratulations!' written on it. I turned to Brad, who was now standing behind me with his arms resting on my shoulders.

"You told them?"

"I sent Suzanna a text when I went to the car to get the champagne."

"Of course you did," I said, shaking my head and smiling. I looked at them all and raised my hands in the air. "I'm a home-owner."

They all cheered and popped the cork on the champagne. The night was set to celebrate the purchase of my very first home. I showed them the brochures of the furniture I had ordered and got a suitable set of ohs and ahs. All in all, the day had been an amazing success. It had been jam-packed with unexpected delights, thanks to Brad.

***

The next day at breakfast I spoke on an impulse. "Suzanna, what would you say to moving in with me while you guys get the permits and plans sorted to build your place?"

Suzanna raised her eyebrows. "Really? You wouldn't mind?"

"Not at all. The place is big. It will give you guys some breathing space because then you won't feel pressured to compromise and get the house built quickly – and I could use the company."

She jumped out of her chair, came over and hugged me. "Yes. Yes, that would be wonderful. Talia, we'd love to."

"We'd love to what?" asked Brad, who had just walked in.

"Talia asked us to move in with her while we're building. She said we could stay as long as we need. Isn't that fabulous?"

Brad smiled. "Thanks, Talia. That would be awesome."

***

I arranged for the property settlement to be executed post haste and organised for all the furniture to be delivered. This was the first time I had placed value in creating a space that was a reflection of me. All the possessions I had in storage in Melbourne were shipped across. Suzanna was an exceptional organiser and had the place in order faster than I could unpack the boxes. It was really nice to have them living with me.

Once we were all settled, I found Mia and Tommy Junior had a habit of waking early and sneaking into my bed. I would lie still, pretending not to notice. They thought it was great to have unfettered access to their aunty. I, too, was surprised at how much I enjoyed being around them. Their eyes of innocence stimulated my creativity, compelling me to dust off my camera once again.

My days were filled with establishing the gardens and riding the neighbour's horses around the property. At night I played with the kids and read them stories. I felt deeply connected to them. It was amazing to witness Brad and Suzanna's relationship. They were perfect for one another. Synchronised to a fault.

On New Year's Eve the family gathered to celebrate the end of an amazing year. Ruth and Shane were pleased to have all of us living close by. This was to be the first time in my adult life that I had spent New Year's in the presence of others. I had always loved the energy of the evening but had never wanted to be lost in a crowd of strangers, and so I preferred entering into the next year in solitude.

This year proved no different.

A few minutes before the stroke of midnight, I found myself standing outside staring into the bonfire. I could hear them inside counting down and then cheering. I smiled. This was going to be a year of giving.

"There you are," said Brad as he approached, champagne glass in hand.

"Happy New Year," I said, returning his smile.

He gave me a warm embrace and rocked me from side to side. "You're going to leave again, aren't you?"

"Yes."

Still in an embrace, he stroked the back of my hair. "Why this time? I thought you were happy."

"I am happy. I want to do something to give back to the world. I need to find a charitable way to make a difference. I have all this money accumulating; it's pointless if I don't put it to good use. I'm going to head across to India. I'm not sure why yet, but it seems like the place to get answers, not that I know the questions, really."

Brad pulled back to look at me. "It's about time the world met you, Talia Jacobs."

I smiled as I touched his face. "You're not going to try and stop me then?"

"You wouldn't stay even if I tried." His voice was sad but accepting.

"There you are. We've been looking for you. Come inside; it's cold. The kids want you to put them to bed, Talia," said Suzanna, waving us towards her.

We walked inside and I read the kids one last story before I tucked them all into bed. I was going to miss those little monsters. They had found a way to entangle their love into the fabric of my being. I was leaving, knowing the next leg of my journey could assist in making their future a nicer one.

India

I found myself overwhelmed with a saturation of foreign smells as I disembarked the plane in Mumbai. It was a thick coagulation of spices, pollution and the distinct smell of human excrement. I didn't know what was worse: the fact I was inhaling microscopic floating particles of faecal matter or that it didn't appear to be as intense by the time I walked across the tarmac to the airport doors. The human body had an amazing ability to adjust. I was equal parts thankful and disgusted.

This was my first trip to India. I had travelled to many places in the world but had not been drawn to visit this space until now. I wanted to witness poverty first hand. I had arranged to have a guide to take me on an expedition to different parts of this sacred country. When I got through customs and had grabbed my bags, I could see a man holding a sign 'Tale Jakob'. I smiled at him to gesture I was the person he was looking for and he responded in kind.

"I am Sandeep, your driver," he said as he reached for my bags.

"That's OK, I'll carry them. I'm Talia. Pleased to meet you."

"No, no, no, I must be helping you with this," he insisted.

I released my grip on the bags and allowed him to place them on the trolley he had beside him. I was in their world now so I needed to adjust to their rules of engagement. Servitude was not something that sat well with me so it would be interesting to see how easily I would adjust.

When we reached the door I was overwhelmed by the fusion of ghastly smells again. I tried not to grimace but felt compelled to cover my mouth and nose. It was a seriously horrible odour.

"AHHHhhhhhhh!" yelled Sandeep at the swarm of beggars that attempted to approach.

"Don't yell at them, please, Sandeep. Don't."

There was a lady holding a baby in her arms. The child had snot running down its nose. Tears streamed from his fly-ridden eyes as she jiggled her body up and down to console him or perhaps encourage him. She smiled as she noticed that I was looking at her child. I could see she used him as her way to obtain sympathy when asking for money. The other two beggars were male. One, an older gentleman, appeared quite deformed. He had three of his limbs severed. The younger fellow had an aggressive facial expression. I assumed his begging technique was to present an air of intimidation. I smiled and waved at them to acknowledge their existence and continued to follow Sandeep to the car. I could hear the airport guards behind me screaming, ushering them to clear the area.

"Beggars are no good. They are rubbish. You must not touch them; they are dirty."

I looked at him and took a deep breath. "It costs nothing to smile, Sandeep."

"They will take all your money. Please no touch the beggars."

I nodded. In essence, I knew what he was saying was true. There would be an endless swarm of beggars following me if they got an inkling I might part with some money. I needed to be mindful of the cultural shift and do my utmost to blend in.

As we drove to the hotel I reflected on my first encounter with beggars. All of them appeared well fed. They had clean vibrant clothes covering their opulent skin. Perhaps these beggars were in the honey spot, hovering on the outskirts of the airport exit. There was an increased probability virginal travellers to India would feel compelled to part with some money. I, on the other hand, was less inclined. I was interested in peeling back the layers to try to understand what made the fabric of a culture tick, aiming to identify opportunity for what could be done differently to make positive change. I wasn't here to assist by tampering with the lives of a few. There had to be a way to provide a repeatable process that could be implemented so poorer communities could help themselves. I placed my belief in the limitless power of imagination.

I had chosen to stay in a three star hotel that offered me a small room with an even smaller en suite. I wasn't planning on spending much time there. In truth, I had suspected the experiences I was seeking from this country of known enchantments might be clouded with conflict, given I was able to afford the luxuries which eluded the majority.

Sandeep and I spent the first few days driving around Mumbai. I wanted to get an uninterrupted visual assessment of the delineation between the richest and poorest spaces. He explained the culture and religious aspects while I listened. It was evident in the words he used he had true pride in his country. I was surprised at how easily I adapted to the acceptance of their strict hierarchy and segregations between the poor, middle and upper castes. From my understanding, Hindus were adamant reincarnation was the cycle of life and the quality of the rebirths was linked to the success of the previous existence. Their belief in arranged marriages was unappealing to me, but I could see by the way Sandeep told of his own experience there was merit and happiness to be found in this process for those who chose to embrace it.

At the end of the first week, Sandeep invited me to his home to meet his family. When we arrived at the sky-rise building I had all eyes on me. The local kids playing soccer stopped and stared. The lady on the balcony hanging her washing off the side of the building also stood still. They made it clear through their demeanour I was on their turf. I felt as though I was walking behind the veil of the unseen. Sandeep ignored them and proceeded into the building with me close behind. We meandered up nine flights of stairs before he stopped at a door, took off his shoes and opened it.

"Mām̐," he called as he stepped over the threshold.

A lovely rotund lady wearing a bright orange, red and gold sari presented from what appeared to be the kitchen area. Using her hand to smooth her hair, she came towards us.

"This is Talia." Sandeep gestured with his hand.

I did a slight head bow and smiled. "Hello."

She walked up to me and placed her right hand on the side of my left cheek. She nodded and then said something to Sandeep.

"Would you like some chai?" he asked.

"I'd love some, thanks," I said, nodding my head.

His mum stepped back and gestured towards the couch. I walked across and took a seat. She disappeared back through the doorway while I assessed the possessions piled in the tiny room. Their lounge room was smaller than my walk-in wardrobe.

"Do you live here too, Sandeep?"

"Yes, my wife, daughter, my grandparents and my brother," he said, swaying his head from side to side.

"It's a nice home you have here."

He walked across to sit on the stool. "Yes, we are very lucky."

I looked about again. It was amazing to think that they had seven people living in this tiny space and considered themselves lucky.

The tea was presented on a tray. I took mine and held it in my hands, wondering whether the water was safe for me to drink. Sandeep's mum waited for me to take a sip. I placed the cup against my lips and took a mouthful. I was grateful it was piping hot and I hoped like hell anything which may have been lurking in it didn't survive the scalding heat that now burnt my tongue.

"What is your mum's name?"

"Shilpa," said Sandeep and his mum nodded.

Raising my cup, I said, "Thank you, Shilpa, it's delicious."

Sandeep translated and she clasped her hands and waved them in response. She addressed Sandeep in Marathi, their native language. After a brief conversation, Sandeep turned to me.

"Would you like to attend my brother's wedding?"

I really disliked attending weddings. To me they were mostly boring. Without knowing what I was getting myself into and not wanting to offend I said, "I'd love to."

"It starts in five days and will last for five days," said Sandeep, once again swaying his head.

"Five days? That's a long ceremony." *Holy shit!*

Sandeep translated for his mum and they laughed. "Yes, in India the weddings are long."

Once I had finished my tea, Sandeep and I left. I wasn't sure why he wanted me to visit his home but assumed he was satisfied I had. His demeanour seemed to alter and he became more like a newfound friend rather than my hired help. When he dropped me off at the hotel he confirmed he had an itinerary planned for the next day. He was starting to take the lead on my adventure and I was happy to let him, for now.

***

In the morning, the first stop was the Mumbai zoo. Sandeep wanted to remain in the car but I insisted he come with me. He had never been inside before. The people who hired him would always leave him in the car park for hours, waiting. It made no sense to me. The entry fee was around one Australian dollar.

I enjoyed watching the expression on his face as he looked at each of the enclosures. His eyes reflected his wonder and I felt privileged to witness it. The allocation of space and the design of the cages was rudimentary and cold. None of the animals showed joy.

I watched as tourists stood in front of the enclosures to get images taken. They were beaming while a depressed lion with little desire for life lay in the background. The apes had eyes glazed over as they rocked from side to side. It was such a disconnection from the spirit they should possess. All these wild beasts were truly trapped in cages. I disliked humanity's need to enclose and control everything for their own entertainment. In hindsight, visiting the zoo may not have been the best idea for me.

"You look angry, Talia," said Sandeep, eating an ice cream I had bought for him.

"I just find the idea of wild majestic animals trapped in small cages profoundly sad."

Sandeep stopped eating and looked across at the monkey enclosure. He thought about my words and then said, "In the monkey cage, there are three living in a space where an Indian family of twenty-five could live happily and still feel they have room for more."

"I understand from your perspective they have a lot of room. These are wild animals who are conditioned to roam free across thousands of acres. Here they are contained by walls; there's nothing to stimulate their minds. They're the living dead."

Once again Sandeep considered my words before he challenged me with his ideas. "They have no enemies here and their bellies are always full."

"OK. Yes, that's true. Tell me, Sandeep. If I place you in a cage with two random strangers, give you no enemies, and provide you the same food daily to keep your belly full, would this make you happy? You cannot interact with anyone else. You have nothing to entertain you. Are you sure this life is lucky?"

He looked at the monkey whose body was slumped over and still. "I would not like this very much," he said. "A man is nothing if he has no family."

"Thank you."

***

The remainder of the day was filled with Sandeep taking me to some local temples. They were not the most interesting spaces for me. I had never been religious and found these buildings stifling, but I lost myself in the beauty of the architecture rather than the crowds of people providing offerings to their multitude of gods. Belief served a purpose for them, not me.

Sandeep took me to a local market. Once again, for a place where food was being handled in large quantities, the smell rising from the steamed ground was ultimately unpleasant. I gravitated towards the caged birds. A small crate held fifty of them crammed together. I was overwhelmed by sadness. I understood that these people would not consider this cruel, yet all I could think of was the gift of flight being stifled in a cage.

"Sandeep, can you negotiate with this woman to buy all the birds?"

He looked across at the stall and then back at me. "A lot of bird would cost a lot of money."

"Yes, that's why I need you to negotiate. She may make me pay double."

"I'll be back momentarily."

I continued to wander the markets. I laughed as a bull meandered past a series of stalls and then bumped into one, pushing over the goods for sale. The stallholders felt it was bad luck to usher cattle away, so they waited for him to leave of his own accord before the shopkeeper cleaned the mess the bovine had left in his wake. Better to be born a cow in this country, I thought to myself.

"Talia, all the birds will cost you a hundred and twenty-five rupees."

"Here's the money. Get all the birds to the car and I'll meet you there in a few minutes. I don't want her to see us together in case she becomes annoyed."

"Thank you very much," he said as he took the money and went off to execute my wishes.

When I got back to the car, there was Sandeep with five crates jam-packed with birds. We estimated there might be over two hundred. We gently placed them in the back seat of the car and drove off.

"What are we doing with these birds?" he asked.

"Let's find a park or some place filled with trees. You and I, Sandeep, are going to free the birds," I said as I patted him on the shoulder.

"Such a lot of money for nothing." He shook his head.

"Sandeep, if you were a bird in one of those boxes behind us, I don't believe you would think it's money for nothing."

He didn't respond; however, I knew he was thinking about what he might afford if he were given such a dowry. I understood my choice to buy the birds would conflict with his personal financial struggles. I just couldn't breathe without trying to redress the balance of entrapment. This was as much for the birds as it was for me.

Sandeep found a lovely spot where we were out of sight of onlookers. We unloaded the car and placed the crates on the ground in front of a group of well-established trees. He used his pocketknife to cut the ribbons holding the lids down. I stepped back and signalled for him to lift the lid on the first box. When he did, a flurry of feathers scrabbled before the first bird managed to take flight up and beyond the trees. One by one they found their freedom. I watched as Sandeep's face lit up looking at the birds circling in the sky while waiting for their friends to join them. Was he now starting to appreciate what I was trying to convey?

I encouraged Sandeep to take the honour of opening all the crates. It was unlikely he would ever experience this again, whereas I was always driven to free caged birds.

One bird remained.

It was unable to fly.

Possibly it had been crushed in all the commotion or through being confined in the box. I could see he was never going to mend. His wings were broken and so was one of his legs.

"Sandeep, do you have a cloth or something I could use?"

"Yes, yes." He scurried back to his car.

He passed me what looked like an old T-shirt.

"Do you need this back?"

He shook his head. "No."

"Don't watch this, Sandeep. Go back to the car. I'll come across in a minute."

He looked at me and then at the T-shirt before turning to go to the car. I leant down and picked up the little bird with the T-shirt. At first it struggled. When I had a clean hold on its tiny body, I swiftly snapped its neck so it could be set free from the binds of its broken vessel.

"Take flight with your friends, little one," I whispered.

I placed the bird's body under a shrub, removing the T-shirt. An animal or some insects would soon feast on its carcass and the circle of life would continue.

Sandeep gathered the boxes and we climbed back in the car before setting out onto the road again.

"See, Sandeep, it's my belief that it's better to be free for one day in flight as a bird than dead in a cage for a lifetime."

"I understand," he said in a sad voice.

"What's wrong?" I asked.

"I'm sad for the bird who did not fly. I am sad that it was you who had to take its life."

"The bird is free of pain, free of constraint and I was the person who gave it the freedom. I consider, in the absence of another choice, it was an honour to help the bird. Don't be sad. It's free."

Sandeep nodded his head to acknowledge my words then remained silent for the rest of the trip back into town and so did I.

The end of the day was drawing to a close. Sandeep took me for a walk through the Mumbai slums. I stood out like a sore thumb and people were obviously wary of my presence. He had assured me he had made the arrangements for my safe passage and I chose to trust him.

This was not a place where thongs were advised. In every space there were piles of steaming divots, and the stench of ammonia from free-flowing urine was overwhelming. It was a mass of corrugated iron sheets making up lean-tos hosting large families in small, dank spaces. The amount of rubbish they tossed in piles on their roofs was a hygiene nightmare. I now understood why Sandeep believed he and his family were lucky. Things could be worse: much, much worse.

In a small clearing in the thick of the slums, a group of women were cooking and some children were playing. They acknowledged Sandeep and stared in silence at me. The fire-women were huddled around the flames and the kids were kicking an empty metal can around like a ball.

"These are my friends. We will stay for dinner," Sandeep said as he gestured for me to step forward.

"I'm not sure they want me here, Sandeep."

"It's OK. Please sit." He pointed to a space near the fire. I crouched down and placed my hands over the flame to feel its heat.

"Hello," I said, scanning the women's faces. They continued to glare at me.

Eventually one spoke. "I am Prita; this is Asha, my sister-in-law; and this is my Aunty Sunita."

I acknowledged each of them and then smiled at Prita. "You speak English well."

Her mouth widened as she released a laugh, nodding her head in agreement. Sandeep positioned himself beside me and placed his hands over the flames too.

One of the kids came around behind me and ran his hand down the back of my hair, saying something.

"He says your hair is golden," Sandeep translated.

I smiled. The little boy thought I had golden hair. I had dyed my hair blonde before I left on my travels, something I had done as a symbol of change. It had never occurred to me that I was entering a world dominated by dark hair, which made me stand out like big-arse dog's balls.

The evening was filled with laughter. We exchanged stories, I played kick-the-can with the kids and was blessed to share a simple meal created to satisfy an appetite, nothing more. I realised, in this place that was considered a tragedy by outsiders, I was in the presence of kindness, witness to a devoted family allegiance and an unashamed expression of love for one another. I received my greatest gift of insight that night.

***

The preparations for the wedding were under way. The festivities were steeped in tradition and the rooms filled with joy. Pratap, Sandeep's brother, had never met his bride. The parents had made the marriage agreement after an astrologer had confirmed they were a match. A union of two strangers was destined to happen in the morning, based on perceived suitability rather than love. It was incredibly hard for me to comprehend. I was fascinated.

As part of the ceremonies I was asked to join in the bride's preparation. I agreed, once again completely unaware what I was getting myself into. The women stripped her bare and she stood naked as the day she was born as they scrubbed her, many hands cleaning sacred places without hesitation. Chandra stood still as they dried her off and then dressed her again. Countless hours were spent drawing intricate patterns with henna on her hands and feet. Her transformation from a simple country girl into a beautiful bride was complete by 3 am.

Later that day, the heart of the ceremony took place. They sat crossed-legged on the floor opposite one another. I was so moved when Pratap lifted the last of the veils that hid his bride's face to reveal the pretty, nubile Indian goddess who was set to be his wife. The expression on his face oozed delight. If I hadn't been a pessimist, I might have suggested I had just witnessed love at first sight. It was magic.

The whole process took a few hours but eventually the rite of passage was completed and these two were now husband and wife. I couldn't help but notice this cool-looking guy across the way who kept staring at me. He was over six foot tall and built like a brick shithouse.

He didn't look Indian. I decided to introduce myself. He watched as I made my way through the crowd towards him and greeted me with a beautiful smile.

"Hello, I'm Talia," I said, putting out my hand out to shake his.

He reached in and gave me a cuddle. "Hi, I'm Haki."

"Your English is perfect," I said, surprised.

He released a big hearty laugh. "So is yours."

I tipped my head to one side. "Are you Indian?"

Tapping his enormous chest, he said, "I'm half Indian and half Maori. My father passed away a few years ago, so my mother moved back here. I've come for a visit and to watch my cousin get married. I live in New Zealand."

I nodded and turned to look at the crowd of people dancing and throwing turmeric at one another.

"Do you want to get out of here?" he asked.

I looked at the cheeky grin on his face and chose not to resist the opportunity. "Sure."

He grabbed my hand and carved a path through the crowd, dodging their attempts to smother us in turmeric. As we made it to a clearing, he glanced at me with a look of satisfaction on his face before continuing to walk. We meandered down the empty street and I noted he was still holding my hand.

"Should I ask where we're going?"

Haki released a cheeky laugh. "I'm taking you back to my place."

I shook my head, smiling at his confidence. "Subtle. Does this caveman approach work with everyone?"

"It does, actually."

We laughed and he shifted from holding my hand to putting his muscular arm around my waist and drawing me closer to him as we continued towards his place.

***

When we arrived, he swung the door open and swooped me off my feet, cradling me in his arms like I was a feather. I squealed in surprise and automatically placed my arms around his thick neck to prevent myself from falling. He kicked the door shut and took me straight into his bedroom, placing me gently on his bed. His body lingered over mine for a divine moment as I felt his breath on my face.

"Wait here," he said as he stood up and walked out the room.

I sat up and looked around the dimly lit space to get my bearings. There wasn't much furniture. Wires used to hang his clothes stretched along one length of the wall. A stool stood in the opposite corner, a towel draped over the seat. Beside the bed was a small table with a lamp. I leant across and switched it on. I could hear him fumbling around but didn't know what he was up to so I waited.

Haki returned wearing nothing but a loincloth to cover his privates. I looked at the tribal tattoos plastered across the right side of his chest, shoulder and upper arm. He carried some items and placed them on the bedside table. I watched him light a small candle, turn off the lamp and open a bottle of oil. This man had a fantastic physique and was undeniably sexy.

"What do you plan to do with that?" I said, reaching for the bottle of oil.

"I'm going to give you a massage," he said as he blocked my hand and gently placed it back at my side.

He stood near the bed and looked at me before walking to the edge near my feet. He pulled my body across so I was lying flat again. Haki maintained eye contact while he gently took off my shoes. He ran his hand up my leg towards my inner thigh, skipped across my midriff and unclasped the brooch holding my sari in place. He had my full attention.

As he removed my clothes, he folded them neatly and stacked them on the chair. When he turned and walked back towards the bed I could see he was aroused. The oil glistened on his hands as he rubbed them together. He dripped the liquid all over the front of my body with one hand as he used the other to place my hands above my head.

"Relax," he said as he positioned himself over my torso.

His warm hands glided along the length of my body in a rhythmical motion. He used his fingers to increase pressure when he drew down towards my legs and lightened his touch on the way up. I closed my eyes to intensify the connection. He kneaded my breasts, worked his hands up towards my neck and across my shoulders, making contact with the full length of my arms and then back down the landscape of my body.

He rolled me over to explore the length of my back. His hands touched every inch of my flesh. I was losing myself in the flow of the movement and didn't notice that he was now kneeling on the bed between my legs. He used the expanse of his fingers to rub up my inner thighs and spread my arse cheeks as he kneaded my buttocks. I could feel myself lifting up as he glided one hand across the length of my spine and ran the other down the cleft of my arse and towards my clitoris. I released a groan as he used his nimble fingers to outline the entrance of my vagina before inserting them. He shifted to lie beside me, his one hand holding my clenched fists above my head, his right leg across my legs to keep them pried apart as he worked his magic with his other hand, exploring the depths of my femininity.

Electric pulses convulsed through my body as I reached the peak of an orgasm that I wished would never end. I wriggled as he continued his exploration, which resulted in me reefing time and time again as my body succumbed to the delights of his persistence. He had magic hands.

I knew Haki was at his threshold of generosity when he turned me over and positioned himself on top. His breath was deep and steady, his eyes were locked to mine as he leant in and clumsily kissed me for the first time. I ran my hands down the outside of his arms and then used my left hand to lightly run my fingers up and down his back. I untied his loincloth, throwing it on the floor, and wrapped my legs around his waist.

At first he gently entered me and started a slow, steady pace. As I lifted my torso to match his movement his momentum increased and he plunged deeper inside me with each thrust. His tongue played with my nipples. I could feel his breath quicken as I reached down and started to stimulate myself. He tilted his head to watch and in a matter of moments buried his face into the arch of my neck and released an elongated groan.

***

In the morning, Haki brought me breakfast in bed. We ate and then continued our intertwined delights. By the afternoon I was begging him to stop. I ached all over and felt decidedly raw from all his attention. I had forgotten how fantastic it was to get lost in a sexual state.

***

When I entered the foyer of my hotel, Sandeep was sitting on a chair asleep.

I placed my hand on his shoulder. "Sandeep, wake up."

He drowsily lifted his head and then jumped to his feet. "Talia, I have been looking for you. Are you all right? Where were you? The hotel receptionist said you didn't come back last night. I was worried."

I felt like a heel. It hadn't crossed my mind to let anyone know that I was leaving the wedding. "Sorry, I left with Haki."

"My cousin?"

"Yes, we left the wedding together last night and it got late so I stayed at his place."

"You are only coming back now?" he said with a raised eyebrow.

I smiled at him. "Yes, I've just returned."

I could see Sandeep wanted to ask more questions but thankfully chose not to.

"I'm going to have a shower and get some rest. I'll see you tomorrow, OK?"

"Are you sure?" He raised his eyebrow again.

"Yes, I'm sure. See you tomorrow." I walked towards the stairwell and headed up to my room.

***

The next day I packed some things into a backpack and headed out the door. Sandeep was waiting in the foyer and to my surprise so was Haki.

"G'day," I said, looking at Haki, who was beaming a wicked smile.

"How are you today, Talia? Recovered from yesterday?" he said with jovial whimsy.

I laughed and looked at Sandeep. "Are you ready for our next adventure?"

"Sorry, Talia, my daughter is sick so I cannot go. I called Haki so that he can take you to Varanasi."

"I'm sorry to hear that, Sandeep. Will she be alright?"

"Yes, yes, yes," he said, diverting his eyes to the floor.

"Sandeep, look at me. Is your daughter really sick or are you just using it as an excuse?"

"Yes, she is sick; very sick indeed," he insisted.

I didn't believe him. I could see by his body language he wasn't telling the truth or at the very least he was hiding something. "OK. Well, please wish her well for me. I guess Haki and I are off to Varanasi."

Sandeep left without saying another word. Haki grabbed my backpack and gestured for me to take his arm. "Madam, shall we?"

I interlocked my arm with his and we headed out the door.

I had heard stories about the Ganges and knew it was revered as holding mystical cleansing powers. When we arrived there I was overwhelmed by the amount of people thronging its banks. They all pushed and clambered to get a position close to the water's edge.

"Why is it so crowded?"

Haki smiled. "Trust me, Talia, this is not crowded."

"Really?"

"During the holy festival this place can have up to thirty million people here to celebrate. There's only a few thousand today. It's nothing in comparison."

I looked across at the people again and squinted my eyes so that their clothing formed a kaleidoscope of colours. It was a melting pot of human flesh of all ages, shapes and sizes. I hesitated to get closer.

Haki reached for my hand. "Come on. I'll keep you safe."

I followed him into the crowd and prayed to the gods he knew what he was doing. I had to accept that in this place personal space was a luxury that no one was afforded. My body brushed up against others and they turned to stare at me. Haki steamrolled forward, parting the people along the way, and they yelled and slapped his arm and back in protest. I kept my head low and stayed close behind him.

When we reached the edge, I looked at the filthy, murky water. There were hundreds of people wading in it, dunking their heads and splashing about. *Ew!*

"Do you want to go in?" asked Haki.

"No, it looks disgusting."

The people behind us were attempting to push forward, so I lost my footing and my feet landed in the water. I turned to try to get back to the edge, without success.

Haki laughed and reached across, drawing me into his torso back on the edge.

I put my arms around him to prevent from falling back again and said, "Thanks."

"I could get used to this," he whispered.

"Used to what?"

"Having you in my arms." He reached down and kissed me gently on the lips.

"Can you take me across to the steps? I think the view would be better and safer from there." I gestured with my eyes where I wanted to go.

Haki waited for me to look back at him before he responded, "Sure, I can do that."

Eventually we made it through to the top of the stairs and found a spot to sit down. In silence we watched the masses of people praying, washing, laughing. The Ganges had been awarded a 'magical' label, but in that space and time I felt it was the people who created the mysticism. If they weren't present, all it would be is just a huge, dirty river. The essence of its beauty was its ability to draw people to its edges.

"What are all those smoke piles I see rising in the crowds?"

Haki laughed. "You may not want to know."

I poked him in the ribs. "Try me."

"They are the funeral pyres of Varanasi."

I tipped my head to one side.

"This is where people get cremated and their remains thrown in the river."

"Oh, I've heard of it, but for some reason thought it was a historical activity. I had no idea that it still happens," I said, now noticing there were smoke clouds rising from everywhere.

"The flames that are used to start the fire are said to have been kept alight for hundreds, some even say thousands, of years. They can have up to two hundred funerals here a day."

"I guess when you consider the amount of people in the country, that's not too many per day. Regardless, it sounds like a fulltime job."

"In India there is a group known as the untouchables. They are born Dom caste, which means they are destined to work throughout their life cremating the dead. That is how they earn their living. It is their job to ensure the pyres continue to burn until the body has transitioned to ash. They control the entire funeral business in this region."

"Can we have a closer look?" I asked.

"Generally women aren't allowed near the Ghats. It is considered bad luck to shed tears over the deceased, so women are banned from being in attendance as they are seen to be more likely to cry. You have to understand, in India death is freedom from this life and a chance to be reborn into another better life. It is a time for celebration not tears."

I stood up, brushing the dust from my backside. "Come on. Let's go bribe someone, shall we?" I offered Haki my hand.

As he rose, he shook his head. "There isn't anything I wouldn't do for you. Are you sure you want to see these bodies close up? It's not nice to witness burning flesh and the smell is horrible."

"Let me be the judge. Come on." I reached for his hand and bravely started to carve a path through the crowd back down the stairs. I was fascinated and wanted to see more.

As we arrived near the Manikamika Ghat, a couple of the Dom approached and said something to Haki, while rudely pointing at me. I waited patiently as Haki spoke to them. After a few heated exchanges, Haki turned to me. "I have to get permission from the Dom Raja. Are you sure you want to do this?"

"I'm sure," I said with no glimmer of hesitation.

"OK, stay here and I'll go with this fellow to speak to the main guy."

"Don't you want me to come with you?" I said, a little concerned.

"I think it would cost more if he saw you. It's better if I go on my own so we can negotiate a decent deal. I won't be long."

"OK, I'll be here."

Haki followed the man between some buildings and then up a street with a steep incline. It didn't take long for them to disappear from my sight. I turned around to look out at the Ganges and noticed a group of men to my right all talking and looking across at me. My presence was clearly not welcome. I remained still, continuing to look forward as they shifted closer to where I stood. My instinct told me to hold my ground. I could feel my blood course through my veins, as they were now almost within an arm's length of me.

I jumped slightly as a loud voice came from behind. The men reacted with expressions of horror, scrambling to get away. They couldn't move fast enough as the voice became louder. I turned and saw an elderly Indian woman fumbling on crippled legs, arms stretched out and reaching forward. Two young women followed suit, also screaming. I assumed they were trying to stop her and had no idea, given the old woman looked ancient and was clearly disadvantaged, how they weren't able to keep up.

As she got closer, I realised her eyes were completely white. There were no teeth in her mouth, except her two top front incisors, which were broken and rotten, and the arms that were stretched out ended in stumps of molten flesh. She stopped directly in front of me, still jabbering in her native tongue.

I studied her face, noting she was smiling.

Her arms reached towards me and she swayed her head from side to side with what appeared to be an expression of joy. I had no idea how she knew where I was positioned, given she was completely blind and I had remained silent.

The two younger ladies caught up. They were out of breath and stood at a distance from the old woman as they yelled at her. She ignored them and continued to speak while waving her decrepit stumps. Warmth exuded from her.

In an unclear moment, I reached out and placed my hands on each of her stumpy arms. In an instant she stilled and silenced her banter. There were gasps from the girls and others who witnessed. I let her arms go and gently placed my hands on either side of her face. She leaned into my hands as if to drink in the moment of a long-awaited touch. I smiled as I felt her purity of being. She was beautiful.

"TALIA, NO!" screamed Haki as he ran towards me.

I yelled back, "Haki, don't," and placed my arms around the woman to protect her.

"She has leprosy; you shouldn't touch her; she is diseased. Please, Talia, let her go."

"Haki, you need to translate for me. Trust me, OK? Please."

"Seriously, Talia, you are playing with your life," he said, raising his voice again, clearly concerned.

"No, I'm not. Ask her to repeat what she was saying to me. I won't let her go until you do this, please."

Haki spoke the words as I released her from my arms so she could respond. It was uncanny how she was able to look directly at him when she spoke. Haki stared at her and then back at me.

"Well, tell me. What did she say?"

"You are the blessed one. You hold the light. She is filled with happiness because she thinks you are here to free her from this life. She wants you to release her light," he said, shrugging his shoulders.

As I turned my head to look at her again she shifted her glance to me and smiled, nodding to confirm her message. I silently pondered what I should do next. Stepping into her space, I placed my right thumb on her third-eye chakra. Her head bent forward into my thumb, increasing the pressure as she placed her stumps in front of her in a praying position.

"Tell her this: she has served this life well. When she sleeps tonight, the light will pass and there will be no pain. As a reward for her servitude, the funeral will be paid for by the light in thanks."

In a soft voice Haki translated my words. She pressed harder against my thumb as she muttered her gratitude. I slowly released the pressure and she responded by straightening her posture. Sending one last toothless smile my way, she turned and headed back the way she had come. The younger women followed at a distance behind her.

"What happens tomorrow when she wakes up?" said Haki, annoyed.

"Sometimes all you need is faith."

"How can you be so sure?" he persisted.

I smiled at him. "I don't have to be. She was, and that's all that matters."

"Can we head back to the hotel? I've had enough excitement for one day. Is that OK?" he asked.

"Sure thing. I need to have a shower," I said.

Haki placed his hands on his hips and tapped his foot. "You are crazy, Talia. She was diseased and rotting. You could catch anything from her. What were you thinking?"

"I just trusted my instinct. I don't expect you to understand but you do need to respect my choices."

We walked back to the hotel in silence.

***

I was grateful for the shower. Haki went out on his own for an early dinner as I had no appetite. I stayed in the room to do some research on the traditions surrounding the pyres of Varanasi. When he returned, we exchanged few words. He was still upset with me.

In bed, Haki held me tight in his arms while we slept. I knew his affections were already starting to develop. Like was quickly transitioning to love and a need to protect.

***

The next day we gravitated to a place where rows of Sadhus sat in meditation. They were devout people who gave up everything to pursue a spiritual path. The core objective was obtaining enlightenment. I was in awe of their varied skills and displays of physical discipline. One man had maintained the same position for years. His limbs where shrunken and his muscles looked like they had atrophied. He did all this damage to his body, which was a gift from god, in order to be entitled to speak with him one day. They spent their lives meditating and reading sacred scriptures. Sadhus renounced ownership of all material possessions, so they relied on people's charity to provide them with food and water. Their devotion to their ideals were admirable.

I sat in front of one of the Sadhus, who was in a deep trance, his eyes open, looking forward and still. I crossed my legs and stared into his eyes. There was an amazing depth to his unfaltering gaze that made me wonder whether he would be able to see my soul. I calmed my breath and watched him watching me, the obstacle in the path of his view. Although I didn't know how to meditate I could feel a level of peace resonate within my core. My thoughts were quiet and everything faded into the distance. I could only see his eyes glaring at me. It was hypnotic.

When I stood up again, I reached into my backpack and grabbed an apple I had taken from the hotel's complimentary fruit platter. I placed it in front of him as thanks for allowing me the shared moment.

Walking down the path away from the holy men, I felt a sense of sadness and awe. The sadness came from my inability to accept that such extremes were ever required by a god, and the awe was of their belief and devotion to try. I accepted this was their choice and knew there was something they obtained by forcing an extreme state that made them hungry for more.

I jumped when I felt a hand touch my shoulder. I hadn't heard anyone approach. Haki also spun around. There, standing before me, was the Sadhu I had just sat with.

He calmly stepped past my comfort zone, looked directly into my eyes and said, "*Jala jīvana kā sāra hai.*"

Haki translated, "He is saying: water is the essence of life."

My eyebrows raised and I smiled at the Sadhu. He returned my smile and walked back to where he had been.

"How weird. I've never seen that happen before," said Haki, scratching his head.

I turned without saying a word. The Sadhu had provided me with the message I was seeking. *Water is the essence of life.*

Our final stop before leaving Varanasi was to head back to the Manikamika Ghat, as I was still keen to have a look at the cremation grounds.

When we arrived, a commotion started as the two ladies from the day before yelled something out and came running towards me. They threw themselves to the ground, touching my feet while others watched in judgement.

I looked at Haki. "I guess the old lady passed last night."

He nodded his head and his eyes widened with disbelief.

"Can you go and pay whomever to ensure she has the best funeral? I want her to have sandalwood, and make sure she's placed face up, not face down," I said.

"What do you mean: face up?" queried Haki.

"In my research last night I read men were burnt facing up and women facing down. I can only assume it is a hierarchy segregation custom. I want this woman to be honoured according to the highest order. She must be face up, OK?"

"Sure, Talia. I'll go make the arrangements now."

I tapped the two ladies on the back, as they were still at my feet. I gestured for them to stand. When they did, I placed my hands in a praying position and bowed slightly. I had no idea what I was supposed to do for them. They may have been grateful or perhaps now they believed I was some sort of deity. It wasn't of interest to me. All I saw in these two women were people who chose to starve their kin of human touch based on an uneducated foundation of fear. I knew from what little I had managed to read the night before that it was commonplace for victims of leprosy to be ostracised from the community. They were often left to starve and die.

Haki returned with two men following. They had serious expressions, which made me think there might be a problem. As I stepped forward, Haki raised his hands to gesture for me to stop. "It's all arranged. These two men will prepare her body while the others build the platform of wood for the fire. Is there anything else?"

"Will they place her face up?"

"Yes. It cost us extra, but they agreed to have her face up."

"Then it's settled. I'd like to stick around to witness her conversion to ashes. Are you OK with that?"

"You know it takes hours for the body to burn?" said Haki.

"It's estimated at approximately three hours. I just want to ensure the head explodes."

"What?" Haki said, surprised.

"They say if the skull doesn't explode then a family member needs to smash it to ensure the soul is set free. I didn't make the arrangements for all of this not to have her soul freed. I want to ensure her death is honoured. It's important for her and therefore for me."

Haki stepped forward and placed his arms around me. He squeezed me tightly and rocked me from side to side. I could hear his heartbeat. I was glad he was here instead of Sandeep. It was nice to share this experience with him, even if he didn't understand.

They created her funeral pile away from prying eyes to ensure they didn't have to explain why a low caste woman was being burnt face up. I didn't mind. I liked the privacy it afforded us. Haki did the honour of lighting the fire while I watched. The heat penetrated quickly. The polluted air was intensified with the aroma of burning wood, incense and a smell like barbecued chicken. There was an occasional waft of something really nasally offensive, which I surmised might be one of the Dom's previous night's curries. Perhaps they thought the spectrum of fumes would mask their wind.

I leant in and whispered to Haki, "Bet you wish you had a blocked nose right about now."

He laughed. "It's certainly an unforgettable smell."

We stood in silence while layers of her body were peeled away by the indiscriminate veracity of the flames. The Dom kept an ever-watchful eye to ensure the heat was evenly distributed. He used a stick with masterly strokes to shift the remains, readjust coals. It was fascinating.

It took a little over four hours for the complete conversion. Haki and I gathered the ashes and threw them into the Ganges and held a moment's silence. I would never forget the joy in her face and the warmth she radiated when I placed her face in my hands. To witness her transition from vessel to ash was an honour.

"Talia, would you have really smashed her skull if it hadn't exploded?"

"You bet I would. No hesitation," I said with a smile.

Haki grabbed my hand. "Let's go home."

***

I spent the last couple of days with Haki back in Mumbai. Sandeep and his family cooked me a celebration dinner on my last night. I gave them copies of the images I had taken at the wedding as a gift for letting me attend. I loved how grateful they were for the simplest of gestures.

Haki drove me to the airport the next day. The whole journey took place in silence. I knew he was considering the prospect of 'us' and was possibly waiting for me to segue into such a discussion. I had forgotten what it was like to be in this position.

I checked in my bags as Haki patiently waited for our moment to talk. I walked across to where he was standing and reached up to put my arms around his enormous neck.

I started, "Thank you for everything. I had a great time."

"It doesn't have to end. I could come to Australia if you wanted me to," he said, kissing my hair.

"I'm headed to America. I'm not planning to go back for a while. There're some things I want to do and the US is where I feel I need to do it."

He didn't say anything; he just squeezed me tightly and then lifted me up to his eye level to kiss me. I closed my eyes and returned his kiss with intensity.

He released a big sigh. "It's a pity. I think you and I could have rocked the Kama Sutra together."

I laughed. "I never understood why it only had a hundred and one positions. It seems so restrictive."

A beautiful smile landscaped his face as he placed my feet back on the ground. "You're going to be hard to forget, Talia."

Gently, I placed my hand on his cheek. "Then don't forget me."

I grabbed my carryon bag and headed to the international entrance. I knew he was watching me, possibly hoping that I would look back, but I didn't. I just raised my hand in good faith, believing he would see me waving as I disappeared behind the doors. That guy fucked like a champion.

Solution Manifestation

The room was overfilled with people. It had taken me the better part of two years to plan and then organise the event. The renaissance-themed charity masked ball had been sold out in less than two days of the exclusive invitations being issued to some of the highest profile and known influential minds the western world had to offer. It was a concept born from my desire to merge the collective genius of a few to create positive change and become an imminent global factor. My idea to create a charity gala at the end of a three-day gathering was surprisingly in higher demand than I had originally anticipated.

The focus of the three days was accessibility and sustainability of nutrition with a primary focus on water being the essence of life. I had invited CEOs from the top Fortune 100 companies, together with people who were leaders in their fields of science, astronomy, astrophysicism, agriculture, permaculture, horticulture, aquaponics, hydroponics, herbalism, homeopathy, biodynamics, invention, philosophy, psychiatry, nutrition, chemistry, pharmacology, cooking and art.

In a room hosting over three hundred people, I stood at the front of the stage with my Madonna-style microphone attached. I could hear myself draw breath as everyone settled and all eyes were on me, a stranger who had asked them to participate in a fully catered event aimed to change the way global issues could be tackled.

I had never addressed an audience before.

"Hello, everyone, thanks for attending what I hope will be the first of many opportunities for us to be together to support an important objective: global access to clean water and nutrition. My name is Talia Jacobs. I am the sponsor and creator of this event that I have called Solution Manifestation.

"I appreciate the time you've taken from your lives to join us. Look around at the people you are sitting next to. They are the leaders in their respective fields. It is unlikely, outside of this event, that you would ever have access to the collective genius that is presented before you. I want to harness the energy in the room to look at providing solution options to make a difference globally.

"Before we begin, I want to remind you that everything already exists and is waiting to be discovered, invented, created or solved. I'm certain you have all experienced enough in your lives to know that rarely is anything as it seems. Alter your perception and your reality changes. In this space I implore you to push past what you know. There shouldn't be limits placed on our imagination.

"There are three hundred of you participating in this event. I have split you into ten groups of thirty. My assistant Michael will join me on stage momentarily to call out the names of each group and what room number you are set to attend. At the end of the day we will reconvene in this room to have a quick debrief before we break for dinner. Thank you again for being a part of this. I hope that it affords the opportunity to influence change on a global scale."

I smiled and bowed before heading off the stage. The crowd clapped their hands. I waved to acknowledge them and patted Michael on the shoulder as he took over the platform and started calling out to the audience.

I was glad my part was over.

As the people dispersed from the large room and headed into their respective sub groups, I sipped my coffee, satisfied. I had been planning this event for over two years. I didn't want to settle for just having access to their minds. I needed them to be invested emotionally. That's why I had designed each room to evoke a visceral response. They were not aware the focus was set on just one country – Haiti. My philosophy was simple – establish repeatable sustainable processes for global nutrition based on the challenges of any one country. Ideally that could form the foundation and methodology, and then ideally only tweaks would be required to align the processes to other countries.

In each group's designated room, I had set the temperature to emulate the current climate in Haiti. Makeshift lean-to shelters were installed to depict Haitian homes, while the quality of the water and the dirt were also present. I had even invited some Haitian representatives, experts in each of the fields, to ensure some of the contributors to the problem-solving were driven by the people who had the greatest vested interest in a positive outcome. I needed their passion to evoke the same in those who participated.

Each room was converted specifically to reflect a key aspect of the challenge that would need to be considered.

The ten rooms of Haiti covered government and politics, religion, education, health, economics, corruption, hygiene, water, climate, and invention. The object was to have people focused on separate aspects so they weren't overwhelmed or deterred by the whole picture. The respective teams just needed to focus on providing sustainable nutrition development plans in the face of their assigned challenge. Solution Manifestation was officially underway.

I spent some time in each of the rooms to see how things were progressing. I felt invigorated by the energy and exchange of ideas. I could see the participants were immersed in the task at hand. It was the first time I had felt a sense of pride. It was nice to feel this way.

At the end of the day we all gathered in the hall once more. A nominated representative from each group presented their challenge and the start of their ideas to remove the obstacles that appeared before them. I was equally delighted with some of the concepts while disappointed at the amount of stifle still evident in some of the ideas. I needed to find a way to fix this.

***

The next morning the group gathered. On their chairs were pen and paper. Once they had settled, I put up a PowerPoint slide revealing the question, "What creature describes you best?"

"Morning, All, before we break up into our groups again, I wanted to run through a little exercise with you to get us started. You all have a pen and paper to write down your answer to: what creature describes you best?" I flipped the presentation to the next slide that had a jumble of words: lion, elephant, mouse, hyena, owl, eagle, snake, buffalo, antelope and bear.

"There are no other instructions. Please put your answer on the paper." I then allowed the slides to flip through powerful imagery of the animals that had been defined. I could see some of the people hesitate; others looked to see what those beside them chose. It was all a representation of stifle.

After a couple of minutes, I said, "OK, please raise your hand if you chose the lion." Some of the people raised their hands. "Thanks. Now who selected the bear?" Once again people raised their hands. "OK, great. Please stand up if you selected a creature that wasn't on the original slide." No one stood up. "Take a look around the room, folks. Not one out of three hundred people chose anything besides what was shown on the slide. That tells me that I'm either a genius and managed to identify the ten species out of the countless millions on this planet you all happen to relate to, or you placed a condition on yourselves to be limited by what was on the slide."

A voice called out from the back, "That's not fair. You never told us we could choose anything."

I smiled. "My exact words were: what creature describes you best? I also stated there were no other instructions. You imposed your limits and conditioned your response based on your own perceptions. I placed no limits on you."

The room broke out into discussion. I could see that they were feeling the impact of the message I was trying to convey. I knew I ran the risk of making them annoyed at the realisation that they were conditioned, but I had to take the risk to help transition to a state of awareness. It was the only way I could assist them in pushing past their restricted state of mind.

"OK. Let's try again. What creature describes you best?"

This time people were less hesitant to write their responses.

"Alrighty, put your hand up if you didn't change your answer." Fifteen or so people in the room had maintained their original choice. "OK, how many of you in the room described yourself in the form of an insect?" No one raised their hand. "Do we have any mythological creatures?"

A gentleman raised his hand.

"Can you please stand up and tell us what creature you are."

"I am Pan, half-man, half-goat, I am the god of mischief and love."

"Well, hello, Pan. I'm thinking you and I might need to catch up later," I said, winking.

The crowd clapped and roared with laughter.

When they settled again, I continued, "Hands up if you would have chosen an insect or a mythical creature had you believed that it was allowed." A few people raised their hands. "Thanks for your honesty. This exercise was designed to show you how our perceived freethinking is bound by the ties of our conditioning. I wanted to place you in a state of awareness so you could approach today's challenges with new eyes in the absence of stifle. We're here to solve puzzles, folks, not to conform within the bounds of problems. I hope this has helped you to feel the presence of your self-imposed limitations. Thanks for participating. You can all head to your assigned rooms. Have a great day."

I finished to a standing ovation. Pausing for a moment, I gazed at the sea of people acknowledging me. I clapped in return and bowed before I walked off the podium and out the side door. It was exhilarating.

I couldn't wait to see what was going to be presented in the afternoon.

***

I spent most of the day with my assistant Michael and the team of workers I had hired to collate the output of the previous day's material. I had graphic designers building the content for the website we aimed to launch at the end of the seminar. It was the age of social media and we were on the cusp of witnessing a boom with platforms such as YouTube, Facebook and Twitter emerging as thought-leaders. I wanted to create a brand associated to a purpose, allowing anyone who was inspired to contribute.

I was delighted with the way everything was piecing together. Amazing concepts, threads to leveraging off existing technologies were being identified. It was a privilege to watch it being collated.

***

On the last day of the seminar, the groups presented their findings. I had Michael take them through the website to show them how their ideas were being captured and shared. The atmosphere in the room was electric. They all beamed with pride at what had been achieved. There was a long road ahead; this was just the start of what was possible.

The evening masquerade gala was quickly approaching.

We all parted ways to prepare ourselves and ready our costumes. This night was set to be filled with magic. Michael had organised my gown for the evening. When I went into my hotel room it was draped across the bed. The material shimmered silver with flecks of pale blue.

The craftsmanship was breathtaking. All the beadwork had been sewn by hand. It was a work of art. I knew this night was one that would be remembered by all who were in attendance.

I stood in front of the mirror as I completed the finishing touches on my hair and make-up. The last item to be placed was my mask. It moulded perfectly to the contours of my face. I felt beautiful.

I headed across to the warehouse early to ensure all the finishing touches were done.

Michael was dressed in his outfit. When he approached me, he bowed and then said, "Wow."

"You too, Michael, you look great. Is everything in place?"

"Yes, I just checked the lighting; the music is set; it's ready," he said with an air of confidence.

I took a deep breath and exhaled. "OK, then."

People streamed through the doors. The costumes and masks were diverse, opulent and sensational. I watched as they looked around the room and pointed at the displays. I was pleased, knowing what they saw was not even a snippet of what was to come. I had let my imagination loose on the concept of this ball and had spared no expense to ensure it would be unforgettable.

All the waiters were court jesters while the waitresses were dressed as Marie Antoinette. I had men on stilts walking about the room blowing flames into the air, actors dressed as nymph fairies throwing sparkled dust around people. The Master of Ceremonies for the evening was Merlin and the security guards were all Knights of the Round Table.

The doors closed as the last of the guests entered the room. People screamed when all the lights went out and the room was blackened. A spotlight switched onto Merlin.

"SILENCE," he yelled in a commanding tone. His arms waved in the air. "Welcome, one and all, to the Gala Masquerade Ball. Tonight there will no reason to take fright, for it ours to embrace in splendour and delight. Take heed, my friends, for there's one thing that's true." He paused as the spotlight switched off and the room became dark once more.

Another spotlight came on to reveal a woman on a swing above our heads. She swung her hand dramatically around her head and in a deep voice said, "Tis a night to be happy, one of joy and play. It happens on this eve but remains in your mind for the rest of your days."

The light went out once more and then shone back on the stage, where a little man was dressed as a pageboy. "It is your masks that hide your face. Be fearless and allow thy truth to be graced. For in this space and time, no judgement will be divined."

The final spotlight lit up a corner where the orchestra was suspended on a platform. They started to play the opening tune and gentle lighting was restored in the room. I walked across the floor to greet my old friend Lena, the lady on the swing.

"Talia, darling," she said with her arms open.

I entered her embrace and kissed her cheek. "Thanks for coming and playing a part. You looked amazing up there."

"I would not miss dis for the world. I live for galas." Theatrically, she threw her head back with her arm across her forehead.

"Is Jean Paul here with too?" I asked, looking at the masked crowd.

"No, his wife is expecting their second child so he could not come."

"Wife? Children? Really?" The last time I had seen Jean Paul in Paris, he was leading the life of a gimp. He wanted only to be in servitude, so it surprised me to hear that he had married.

"Yes, you are bad for business, Talia."

We both laughed.

"Is Enzo here?" I asked.

"He is getting some drinks for us. He will return momentarily."

"I have to mingle. I'll find you later so I can say hello to Enzo too," I said.

"Go. You cramp my style, anyway," she said with a cheeky smile.

I walked around the room and spoke to guests at random. They were all having a wonderful time. The professional dancers were executing a modern take on traditional ballroom dancing. I had also hired instructors to encourage people to participate in the tradition. Watching from the sidelines, it seemed to be a success.

"Madam, may I have this dance?" asked a gentlemen, who held his arm out for me.

I placed my hand on his arm. "Sure."

He led me to the centre of the floor, where he swiftly put me in the correct position. The last time I had danced was the salsa with Ethan. It seemed like a lifetime ago. I tried my best to accept this man's lead. I had an awful habit of trying to preempt moves. The repetition of the dance allowed me to find my footing easily. He lifted his arm to gesture I turn and then left me in the presence of another, as the dance required a swap of partners. I clumsily placed my hands in position. As my new partner intertwined his fingers in mine, I felt an electric pulse run through my core. I looked beyond the mask into his deep blue eyes. He had a wry smile that harboured secrets. In silence, he returned my gaze and we danced.

When the music stopped, he bowed. "Thank you for the dance. I'm B."

"Billy, Billy, there you are. I've been looking all over for you," said a lady in a dramatic bird mask with an elongated beak.

I smiled. "Thanks for the dance." I turned and walked off the dance floor. I needed a drink.

The bartender poured me a Frangelico on ice. I turned to lean against the bench as I took my first sip. In the distance I noticed an elderly tribal woman who was not in costume. She stared at me as I puzzled over her presence. She seemed so familiar but I couldn't place her in my mind.

"You see her too," said the lady who appeared beside me.

I looked at her. "Why wouldn't I see her? She's right there."

"She's not of this world. She comes with a message. I think it's meant for you," she said, peering past her mask.

"You're Flore, yes?" I asked, recognising the Haitian woman's voice.

"Yes, Talia, I am she," she said, looking surprised at my ability to recall her name.

I scanned the room and couldn't see the woman in tribal dress anymore. When I turned to my left, she was standing near the exit.

"She wants you to follow her," said Flore.

The elderly woman nodded when Flore said those words. I skulled the rest of my drink, placed the empty glass on the bench and walked across to the elder. She proceeded out the door, so I continued to follow.

She led the way to the conference rooms, where she walked up to a map of Haiti. She pointed to Port-au-Prince.

"You want me to go to Haiti?" I asked.

She smiled and reached across, placing her warm hand on my heart, speaking only one word, "Marlee."

Marlee

I arrived at the airport and was greeted by Edgard, Flore's husband. She had kindly arranged for him to pick me up and help me in my search to find Marlee. The last time I had been here I was six years old. At the time, it was the only home I knew and Marlee was my nanny. She watched over me as if I was her own. She stood by me through my darkest hours and I assumed that her summoning me was to return the favour. Time was of the essence.

Edgard and I went to the local police station to ask if they knew of her. They laughed at us when we told them the name, suggesting there were many people of that name they could introduce us to. I went across to the Union School that I had attended as a child in the hopes I could retrace the path back to the house we had rented. I drew a blank. There was a sense of familiarity but my mind was clouded. I couldn't identify anything that I could use as a marker for me to follow.

I stayed with Edgard that night and played with his beautiful children. Before I laid my head on the pillow, I whispered to the universe, *Guide me to Marlee. Show me the path I do not see.* I slept like a baby and woke in the morning without any vision of where I needed to go.

"Edgard, let's just get in the car and drive. I need to find her."

"Do you know which direction?" he asked.

"No, but I will. We just need to go."

He said goodbye to his kids, leaving them in the care of their aunty. We got in the car. I pointed in a direction and we headed down the road. As we left the urban landscape behind us I could hear the distant sound of drums.

I looked across at Edgard. "Do you hear that?"

"No, I don't hear anything. What do you hear?"

I repositioned myself in my seat. "Drums. I hear drums."

He listened and then looked across at me. "No, I don't hear anything."

I smiled. We were heading in the right direction. I knew it.

The beat of the drums increased as we continued on our route. In the distance I could see a car broken down on the side of the road. As we drew near, a man waved his hands for us to stop. Edgard slowed the car and scanned the area. I could see he was hesitating.

"What are you looking for?" I asked, following his gaze.

"Looters. It is not safe out here." His voice held concern.

The area seemed to be clear. Against his better judgement, Edgard pulled his car to the side of the road and got out to assist the man. As he drew closer, the boot popped open and two men jumped out brandishing machetes.

"Out, out!" screamed a man with wild eyes, staring at me.

I carefully got out of the car.

Edgard had been pushed to his knees and a man was yelling at him in a native tongue while slapping him hard across his head. There were three men in total and they looked enraged.

Edgard slowly stood up and started walking back towards the car. He paused to look at me. "I have children." He jumped into the car and drove away.

The looters waved their large knives, laughing at me. I carefully looked around to see if there was anything I could use to defend myself. If I tried to run and they caught me, I would compromise my ability to fight. I had to stand and not show fear; I didn't want to increase their pleasure.

"Ehhh, NO," yelled the crazy-eyed man, indicating I had to face forward.

One of the other men walked across to me and picked up some of my hair and smelt it. He smiled back at the other two and said something that made them laugh. I kept still and watched them. I knew they were inclined to gang-rape, possibly killing me afterwards or leave me for dead. Still, they had let Edgard go, so perhaps their intent was just rape.

There was movement in my peripheral vision. I shifted my gaze subtly to see the elderly woman was present. She had stillness about her. She didn't seem to be concerned about my current predicament. I watched as she raised her arms and placed her hands behind her neck. *Did she want me to do this?* She nodded, confirming the answer to my unspoken question. I looked back at the men, who were now arguing, possibly over who was to have the honour of going first. I took a deep breath, tried to silence my thoughts, slowly raised my arms above my head and clasped my hands behind my neck.

One of them looked across at me and said something to the others. They all stared. Their expression changed to what looked like fear. I maintained my position. They pushed the smallest fellow towards me. He hesitated before slowly approaching me to inspect my right arm.

His eyes widened and he jumped back. "Voodoo."

I looked at the elderly woman. She was smiling.

One of the men closed the boot and they all jumped into their car. They drove off, leaving me in the wake of their dust. I smiled. They feared the tattoo that I had placed under my arm. It was the voodoo symbol of Papa Legba, representing the keeper of the crossroads between the human plane and the spiritual. Marlee had packed this symbol in my bag just before I left Haiti. I had carried it with me for years. The paper had gradually worn during the course of my travels, and I had it tattooed onto me so I could have it with me always.

The elder walked over to me and placed her hand on my cheek. I nodded. She turned and headed down the dirt road. I followed, marvelling at the surreal experience. I had never had my life threatened before. I was not sure how I would have reacted if I'd had the misfortune of being attacked and harmed. A level of latent rage surfaced and I knew I needed to contain it.

I could hear the sound of a vehicle approaching. I moved off to the side and wondered whether the three were returning to finish what they had started. As the sound grew louder, I recognised Edgard's car. It screeched to a halt and he jumped out and hugged me. There were other men with him, who also got out of the vehicle.

"Are you OK? Did they hurt you?" he said as he inspected me.

"No, they left without touching me."

He looked at me, puzzled. "They said they were going to hurt you and kill you. They said I had to leave or stay and die. I left to get help. These men are from Marlee's village."

"You found Marlee? This is great. Let's go."

I headed to the car. One of the men opened the front passenger door for me.

As we drove down the road, I thanked the others for coming to my aid. They had been willing to place themselves in danger to help a stranger. Their kindness was not lost on me.

"Talia, these are Marlee's sons," said Edgard.

I turned my head to look at them. "Wow! Marlee had children. That's beautiful. I'm Talia. Your mum looked after me when I was very young."

"We know. Mum spoke of you often," said the one sitting in the centre.

It amazed me to think I had made such an impact on her, enough to carry thoughts of me through the passage of time. It was a reminder of our ability to influence and have impact simply because we exist.

"Talia, I am sorry I stopped to help him." Edgard paused for a moment and then said, "I left you."

"It's OK. You did the right thing. There was no need for both of us to die. You were right to go; you have children." I placed my hand on his arm and squeezed it.

He pursed his lips and gulped for air as he started to cry. I looked at the road ahead and kept my hand on his arm. He had been placed in a horrible position and I could appreciate he was overwhelmed by guilt. I didn't begrudge his decision to leave. I was relieved he had. As scary as it was to be left there, I would have been devastated if something had happened to him because he was trying to help me. Once again I could feel a bubbling rage trying to surface.

Crowds of villagers swarmed the car when we arrived. They were all anxious to see we were OK. I felt exposed. I was the keeper of secrets and the experience was something I didn't care to share. I wanted to leave it behind me.

A lovely lady with a warm glow about her came over to me. "I will take you to Marlee. She has been waiting."

I walked with her hand-in-hand through the laneway to a bright green door. The woman paused before she opened it. "She's dying. She waits for you."

"I know," I whispered as my anger was replaced by sorrow. Tears fell from my eyes. No experience in life ever prepared you for saying goodbye.

We went inside. She was lying on a bed with a white sheet covering her body. Flowers lay on the floor around her. She was sleeping. The lady quietly brought a stool into the room and placed it near me so I could sit. Then she left us. There were hundreds of burning candles scattered around the room. Their flames were still. I reached under the sheet, found Marlee's hand and held it.

In her slumber she seemed at peace. She looked beautiful. I was thankful for her absence of pain. I had no idea why she was dying; I just knew she was. Calming my breath, I stared into the flame of a nearby candle. Its transient light was hypnotic and charmed my eyes. Soon I found the rest of the room faded into black and all that was present was the flame and the sensation of holding Marlee's hand.

I heard a voice in my mind. *You came.*

"Yes," I responded in a whisper.

Thank you, said the inner voice. *I want to show you.*

Images started to appear in the flame, unwinding from a reel like an old homemade movie. I saw a man holding Marlee's hand. He was courting her. The images skipped to Marlee being wedded. I saw the ring being placed on her finger and the look of delight on her face. My eyes filled with tears when hands held up a newborn baby. It repeated three times to represent her sons. Marlee was showing me a reel of her life. I watched in wonder as she presented to me all that I had not been here to witness. I couldn't believe that in her final hours she was insisting on giving me this gift. One beautiful moment melted into another. She had lived a truly blessed life.

Marlee gently squeezed my hand as the images shifted to my childhood. There I was, a little girl being lifted and spun in my father's arms, my mother cradling me in her lap as she read me a story. Me walking down the street with Marlee and a little boy. I was overwhelmed with emotion but dared not blink, as I didn't want to stop seeing. Then I saw an image of two men on a porch. I looked at the face of the man smiling at me and realised he was the same person that Marlee had married.

Yes, said the voice.

I responded, "You married the police officer?"

Yes.

I released large sobs as I realised that Marlee was showing me something good had come from my parent's death. She had met the man of her dreams and they had created a life together. This was why she talked of me often. She credited her joy to having known me. It was a perfectly beautiful sentiment that I wanted to embrace.

As I cried I spoke in my mind, *Thank you, Marlee. I will be forever grateful. Thank you.* My six-year-old inner child surfaced and I cried hysterically. The images in the flame faded and the room became visible again. Marlee squeezed my hand before releasing her final exhale. I leant across her torso, weeping as I had never done before.

The front door opened. One by one the villagers came into the room, humming a tune. They gently placed their thumbs on Marlee's forehead and did the same to me. My face contorted with tears of pain and simultaneous joy to be witness to such overwhelming beauty. Her sons were the last to enter the room. They executed the same gesture and then raised me to my feet. I released Marlee's limp, cold hand and turned to look at them.

One by one they held my head and leant in so our foreheads touched. "Sister," was the only word spoken.

There was no consoling me now.

***

The next six days the villagers mourned over the body. The elders prepared Marlee for the burial, which took place on the seventh day. She was to be laid to rest in a grave beside her husband Cedric. Her sons carried the coffin to the hole freshly dug into the earth, lowering it into the ground steadily with ropes. I quietly watched as the villagers all took turns in shovelling the dirt to cover her.

She was well loved by all.

Darkness

I returned to the US feeling a greater sense of purpose. Michael had led the team in my absence. The response to the launch was extraordinary. People from everywhere were contributing their ideas to the cause. An entire room at the back of the office was filled with letters and packages waiting to be opened.

Michael pointed to an open pile. "You should read these."

He looked amused as he watched me pick up the first letter.

I read the words and looked back at him. "It's a proposal of marriage."

"Yep," he said with a laugh. "They all are."

"For real?" I was in disbelief. "That's bizarre."

"You have one hundred and twenty-three so far, and we still have all these to open, so I expect there will be more," he said.

"It's amusing and kind of sad." I placed the letter back on the pile and walked towards the door.

"Aren't you going to read them?" he questioned.

"No. That, my friend, is your job. Get one of the girls

to compile a nice response to tell my suitors their message has been received and respectfully declined."

I walked out and Michael followed me into my office.

He waited for me to be seated. "We've been getting requests from different media groups for an interview. Do you want to go through the list and see which ones you want to do?"

"Bring me the list and leave it with me. I'll go through it and get back to you."

"OK." He left.

The idea of being in the public eye didn't appeal to me. I wasn't shy or concerned about speaking publicly. I just didn't want things to revolve around me. The cause had to stand on its own. I understood the media involvement would contribute to the cause in a positive way when managed correctly. I needed to find someone who could be the face of Solution Manifestation.

"Excuse me, Talia, your lunch appointment has arrived," said Michael, standing at the door.

"What appointment?" I said, looking at my calendar.

"It's in there. His name is Blake Quark. He was one of the contributors at the seminar."

"Do you know what it's about?"

"No, he called a few times while you were in Haiti and then booked this appointment."

I didn't hold back my look of annoyance. "Bring him in."

Michael left and returned post haste with Blake in tow.

I stood and walked over to meet them halfway. "G'day, Blake."

"Hi, Talia. You're a hard woman to catch," he said, accepting my handshake.

"Indeed, I am an elusive creature. Please take a seat." I gestured to a chair.

"Actually, I wanted to take you out for lunch, if that's OK."

Michael stood behind Blake, smirking.

"That will be all thanks, Michael." I glared at him until he left.

"Lunch it is," I said to Blake as I grabbed my bag and we headed out the door.

***

At the restaurant we made small talk while we placed our order. When the waitress returned with our wine, she poured some into my glass for me to test. I waved my hand, gesturing it would be fine, so she filled our glasses and then left.

"I've never had that happen before," he said, looking at my wine glass.

I laughed. "I've never had it happen any other way." I knew he was referring to the waitress choosing me as the person to do the first taste of the wine.

"You have an amazing presence about you. I bet people gravitate to you like flies."

I'm sure his words were intended to be a compliment but mostly I felt disheartened at the thought that people saw something in me they chose not to see within themselves.

"I have my moments but I'm sure you didn't ask me out to lunch to talk about my presence. What would you like to discuss?" I said, looking into his eyes.

"Small talk time is over, right?" he said, slightly amused.

Maintaining eye contact, I returned his smile and sipped on my wine in silence.

He started. "I attended the seminar."

"I remember. You're Pan, the god of mischief and love."

"Wow, good memory."

"There are moments when it serves me well. So you attended the seminar and …?"

He looked down at his glass of wine for a moment and then his tone changed. "That seminar had an impact on me. I'm a bio-physicist by trade. I built my company from the ground up and have been very successful. Those three days made me realise I wanted to be more than a successful businessman. I want to be part of something greater. I want to work with you on developing Solution Manifestation."

"What are you proposing?" I said, not altering my gaze.

"Money isn't an issue for me. I'm a wealthy man. I've appointed my second in charge to run the company so I can free up my time to work with you. I'm not looking to be hired. I'm looking to contribute."

I looked down at the napkin in front of me as I considered his words. He waited patiently for me to respond. I did my best to choose my response carefully. "I have to ask. I have a lot of people motivated to be around me, secretly wishing I'd become more to them than just a work colleague or friend. When you say you want to work with me, is it purely for the united belief in what we're trying to achieve or more?"

He smiled as he reached into his pocket and pulled out a ring. "I'm a happily married man. My intentions are pure."

I nodded. "What are your thoughts on public speaking?"

He raised an eyebrow and smiled. "I love it."

I reached across and offered him my hand. As we shook, I said, "Welcome on board, Pan. You are officially appointed as the face and voice of Solution Manifestation."

"Isn't that a role you should own? You're the one who created this concept. Don't you want to get the credit for your efforts?" he asked.

"Absolutely ... Not. No credit required or desired. The further I'm placed away from the public eye the better as far as I'm concerned. It's all yours. I'II be the puppet master and you will be the puppet, except no one will ever know. It's perfect."

He winked. "I'm not too sure about the puppet analogy but I'm excited to be on board and would love to represent the cause."

***

Blake spent the next twelve months campaigning and spreading the word while I worked with the team on the ground to develop a strategy for supplying clean water to poor districts in Haiti. The team extended to include lawyers, political advisors and cultural experts.

The founder of a charity group called H2O Water Wise approached us to discuss assisting the cause. They were currently making a difference in areas of Africa channelling and drilling for water so a direct source was available in villages. They wanted to expand but their funding was limited. We merged forces and mapped out our first of five villages in a district outside Port-au-Prince to kick off the project.

There was excitement in the air as the team arrived in Haiti. All the equipment required for drilling was purchased and en route to the villages. Volunteers from around the globe attended to offer a hand. We hired people from the local villages to be part of the team. I felt it was important to be inclusive so the positive developments would engender a sense of pride in the community. It would increase the probability of the wells being maintained after we were gone.

While the project was getting underway I flew across to the UK to meet with a man called Tom Brineheart, who had invented a filter system for water bottles and jerry cans that removed dangerous microscopic particles, making polluted water safe to drink. The preliminary tests had indicated the filters could last for up to a year. The concept was exciting because it would provide people with cleaner water immediately.

The field results spoke for themselves. The challenge was the price point for developing the product. I reached out to Sandeep in India to get him working on establishing some manufacturing contacts for Tom to speak to. We had to find the most economical way to mass produce the items without compromising the quality.

I continued to fly around the globe to meet with people who had something to offer in the way of water quality improvement and hygiene. The intelligence being gathered increased the hope that we could make an incredible difference. The only factor that remained a challenge was the finances to obtain and sustain the supply of these products.

I flew across to Haiti to visit the team.

The exploration drilling was proving difficult. They were going deeper underground than they had initially anticipated. The water table was either low or they weren't in the right spot. The foreman assured me this was not unusual.

Blake was on site with a camera crew to record the activities. This material was being passed back to Michael and the team so it could be loaded onto the YouTube channel. All the sponsors and donors received updates regularly so they could be part of the journey. We wanted to ensure people could witness how they were contributing to the difference being made.

We had to hire armed guards to ward off looters. There had been an increase in attacks on the villagers. I could feel the tension in the air. I was concerned for the volunteers and wanted to ensure we did everything possible to maintain civility.

Wilfred, one of the armed guards, escorted Blake and me to Marlee's village. I wanted to visit my brothers. Upon our arrival, the children gathered at the doors and opened them, playfully calling out with their arms in the air.

"Hello, little ones," I said, tapping their hands.

The elders appeared from behind their doors and came out to greet us. I hugged them and laughed as they touched my face. My three brothers, Toussaint, Dieujuste and Josias, soon followed and embraced me in a group hug.

"These are my friends, Blake and Wilfred."

They looked at the gun that Wilfred was carrying.

"It's OK. We had some problems in the village where we're working so I've hired armed guards to keep the looters away." It hadn't crossed my mind they might feel uncomfortable in Wilfred's presence.

"We must celebrate," said Toussaint.

The kids screamed their approval. The elders scurried to organise things while we went to visit Marlee's grave.

They had placed a headstone at the site, which said, "Marlee Miot, Wife of Cedric, Mother of Toussaint, Dieujuste, Josias, Talia."

I silently stared at my name carved in stone.

Josias stepped in, placing his hand on my shoulder. "Sister."

When we rejoined the others, the villagers had already set the tables, the fire was in the process of being lit and the drummers were setting up their rudimentary instruments.

I looked across at Blake. "You're in for a treat. These guys know how to party."

Wilfred smiled. He knew exactly what I was talking about.

***

The celebrations were under way. The women danced and the men talked and drank. I listened to the hypnotic rhythm of the drums and felt at home. Haiti had provided me with the best and worst of my experiences. I loved these people and what they represented to me: community.

***

The next day we got back on the road to return to the project. A few miles past the village, I felt a sense of dread as we approached a car parked on the side of the road. There were four men huddled over something in the clearing.

I screamed, "Stop the car," and opened the door.

Wilfred slammed on the brakes as I jumped out. I ran towards the men. Three of them stood up and came towards me. I didn't hesitate. I maintained my momentum and with all the force I could conjure punched the man closest to me in the face and swiftly kicked the inside of his knee to disable him. He fell to the ground, screaming in agony and grasping his leg.

The other two men dispersed when they saw Wilfred running towards us, armed. He released a shot into the air as a warning. The fourth man was on the ground, his pants halfway down his legs and beneath him was the small child he was raping. In a blind rage, I reached down and yanked him off and onto his back, before stomping my foot on his abdomen. As his body reefed forward, I kicked him in the face and then with both legs jumped on his chest as hard as I could. Every ounce of my being wanted him dead.

Wilfred grabbed my arms and pulled me back, but I fought to be released to continue my attack.

"You killed him," Wilfred said.

I looked down at the still body. I shuffled out of Wilfred's grip to check. The man was still breathing but unconscious. Two of the men had escaped and the third lay writhing on the ground, clutching his injured knee. I was still enraged. I wanted them all to feel my wrath.

My fists clenched as I screamed, "FUUUUUUUUK."

I dropped to my knees beside the limp body of the little girl. She was so badly beaten that I couldn't see her features through the blood and swelling. I gently lifted her head to check she was breathing. Her little hands were bound with rope. She was so tiny.

I reached out to Wilfred. "Give me your knife."

He bent down and freed the child from her binds, not trusting me to hold a weapon. That was a smart move on his part.

"Throw these two in the boot." I pointed to the injured men.

Blake, pale as a ghost, slowly came forward. "The boot might not have enough air for them."

I glared at him. "Do I look like I give a fuck? Stick them in the boot or kill them and leave them here. We have to take her to hospital."

They did as I instructed, placing both men in

the boot. Wilfred then gently picked up the little girl and placed her across the back seat of the car with her bloodied head resting on my lap. We headed down the road at full speed.

"You could have been killed. I was so fucking scared," Blake said in a whisper.

I didn't respond. I stared out the window in a silent rage that I couldn't contain. Adrenalin was surging through my body. My hands shook and I felt cold. I hated these men. I wanted them to suffer. If Wilfred hadn't stopped me I would have killed that wretched man. I hated him to the core of my being. She was only a child.

I had never spoken to anyone about my brush with the same fate and it had left me feeling vulnerable. Months after, I still saw the images of my attackers, smiling. I had vowed I would never allow myself to feel like a victim again, so I had hired a mixed martial artist to train me in street combat. Over the last year and a half I had been training with him three times a week and on my own every other day for three hours a night. If there were to be a next time I wanted to be prepared. I would kill or be killed.

Blake called ahead to the hospital and notified the police, so when we arrived they were waiting out the front with a gurney. Swiftly they took the little girl inside to theatre. I stood there numb and silent while Wilfred spoke to the police officers as they walked to the boot to release the men. Both needed medical attention. They were taken in by the medical staff with police guards to supervise.

"Who beat the men?" asked one of the officers.

"I did," responded Wilfred.

The police officer looked across at me, noticing my

hands were shaking and bloodied. He then glanced at Blake, who was sitting on the kerb with his head in his hands.

"What of the other two men?" he continued.

"They ran away when I shot my gun in the air to scare them," said Wilfred.

The police officer came across and reached down, grabbing my hands. I let him. He inspected them and then looked into my eyes. I stared back at him without speaking a word.

Wilfred stepped in. "She has blood on her hands and clothes because she held the girl."

This seemed to satisfy him. He released my hands and walked inside the hospital to speak with the two men.

"Talia, the police cannot know that you did this," Wilfred said with concern.

I still couldn't speak. I felt disconnected from all emotion. I needed to settle the rage that flowed through my core.

"The men will never admit that a woman beat them. It would bring shame." Wilfred shifted his position to gain my eye contact. "You will be safe."

I blinked to acknowledge what he said while thinking about the word *safe*. Satisfied with this, Wilfred went to check on Blake, who was now leaning against the hospital wall, throwing up.

The surgery to repair the internal damage the little girl had sustained took three hours. The police were not able to identify who she was so we had to wait for her to regain consciousness.

Three days passed before she finally woke and by that time the police had already found her parents. As they arrived, I left her bedside without saying a word.

When I rejoined the others, Wilfred confirmed the

other two men had been captured and now all four were being held in custody. He told me they would only get three months in jail at most although it would have been more if the girl had died.

***

The next day, through Wilfred I made secret arrangements to visit the jailed men on my own. I walked into the holding bay, where they were sitting in a row on a bench. An armed guard stood beside me. I stared through the bars at the men in silence and they glared in contempt back at me. The one I had beaten unconscious spat on the floor. Their smiles turned to expressions of pleasure as they watched the tears roll from my eyes. I accepted they had no remorse. I nodded my head to acknowledge their position. I reached under my top and pulled out an envelope. It contained a thousand US dollars. I tapped it on the bars to show them and then placed it in the guard's hand.

"Beat them. Every day, beat them."

The guard held his gaze in place, only moving his arm to put the envelope inside his jacket.

I left in the knowledge that I would never forget their faces and now they would never forget mine.

Healing

I recognised I needed to regain a sense of self. My life was filled with a roller coaster of experiences that took me to the lightest and darkest of spaces. I could no longer maintain a sense of balance and I knew it had to be addressed. I wouldn't allow myself to be consumed by anger over injustices I had witnessed. I had to love myself more than that.

It had been six weeks and Blake was still visibly shaken by the experience. He sought the assistance of a therapist to help him process what had taken place and to work through his acceptance of his role. He implored me to do the same but I didn't see the point in speaking about something I could never change. I had no regrets and felt no shame in the choices I had made.

Some time later, Blake walked into my office. "Talia."

I looked at him and smiled. "Hey, what's up?"

"I just spoke to Wilfred. He told me the four men died last night. They were beaten to death by some inmates." His face was pale and his hands were shaking.

I pursed my lips and turned to stare at the view outside my window.

"I thought you should know."

"Thanks," I said, not altering my gaze.

"I know you don't want to talk about it but I really need to. I think it would be good for both of us." He shifted to block my view. "Talia, please. I'm worried about you."

"I'm fine. There's nothing to worry about," I said.

"Well, I'm not. Help me understand what happened. I need to talk this through and I think you're the only one who can do it with me."

I rubbed my face, frustrated at the idea of discussing the event. I was still very raw and had not put to bed my own thoughts about the experience. Still, this was not just about me. Blake was clearly struggling. I had to extend beyond my needs to do as he asked.

"Let's go for a walk," I said as I stood up.

I took him to a park and we sat on the bench. I stilled my breath while Blake patiently waited.

"I went to Haiti straight after the gala to visit a dear friend who was dying." I paused to inhale a deep breath.

"I was being escorted by a fellow, Edgard. He was the husband of a woman who participated in the seminar. As we drove down that same road there was a car parked on the side with a man waving us down. We stopped. When Edgard approached him, two men jumped out of the boot carrying large knives. They beat him to his knees and then screamed at me to get out the car."

The image of the men was present in my mind again. My heart pulsed faster; my hands were starting to shake. I clasped my hands in an attempt to still them.

"They told Edgard to leave or die, so he left me. He has children. I have never felt more alone than in that moment as I listened to the sound of his car driving away.

They tormented me with their laughter. I was scared. I was angry. I was frustrated. When one of the men came across and sniffed my hair I knew death would be a kindness in comparison to what they had planned."

Blake reached across and placed his hand on my knee. "I'm sorry, Talia. I didn't know."

"Don't touch me," I whispered.

He removed his hand and sat still.

"The men never harmed me physically. Years ago I branded myself with a tattoo of a powerful voodoo symbol and thankfully when they saw it they were scared of it. In fear, they left me there and drove away as fast as they could."

Blake released a sigh of relief. Given what he had witnessed with the little girl, I knew he was imagining the worst for me.

"Walking down the road alone, I felt the depth of my anger. I was enraged at them but my anger was directed at myself. I felt weak and vulnerable and I hated it. I had strength of mind unmatched by any I have met in this life, but my body was weak. When I returned to the US I trained relentlessly in mixed martial arts. I wanted to ensure I never allowed myself to feel helpless again."

I paused to watch a duck and her young swimming in the lake in front of us. The mother called constantly and checked to see they were all present. I smiled when I saw one of her babies had nestled into the soft down on her back. It was fast asleep, safe, warm, loved.

"When we were driving down that road and I saw the car on the side, I felt those same emotions of dread and terror. Images of what had happened to me flooded my mind. As we travelled past, I saw a foot facing upwards under the men. It sent me into a blind rage. My adrenalin took over as I ran towards them and did what I did. I had no idea it was a little girl. That just made it worse."

"You saved her life. If you hadn't made us stop the car, she would be dead."

"That's just it, Blake. I wasn't saving her life. I was resurrecting mine." The tears came as I stared into his eyes.

He started to cry too.

I placed my arm around him; he leant across and sobbed deeply into my shoulder. I recognised a familiarity in his pain. His struggle was because he had frozen while the event took place. He had sat in the car while I fought the men and Wilfred ran to my aid. He felt like a coward. That's what was eating him.

I held him in my arms as he continued to wail, rocking him gently and stroking his back. It was in the face of life-threatening events that you were witness to who you are rather than who you imagined you would be. The misalignment between ideals and reality were not the most pleasant introduction to a state of self-awareness. I had been there and lived the dream. Blake and I now had a relatable experience that had different outcomes for us both.

"Talk to me, Blake. What are you struggling with?" I prompted.

"I froze. I was so scared I couldn't move," he whimpered.

"It wasn't your fight, Blake. It's normal to be scared. You have nothing to be ashamed of."

He buried his face deeper into my shoulder.

"Don't hide. Look at me." I placed my hand under his chin and lifted his head so I could see his face. His eyes were bloodshot, his lashes stuck together, and the sun highlighted the path his tears had taken on the contours of his face.

"You're punishing yourself. Don't let this experience sabotage your love and self-respect, or they win. Learn from it. The first time round, my looming regret was that I was physically weaker than I imagined in my mind. I'm not deluded that learning to fight made me invincible. I did it because I understood I would have regrets if I allowed these perpetrators to make an easy meal of me. If I was destined to die under such circumstances, I wanted to provide my best fight. My physicality had to match the strength of my mind. That is what I learnt about me the first time around."

Blake sat up. He stared at a patch of grass in front of his feet. "You weren't afraid."

I bent my head down so my face was in his peripheral vision. "No, I wasn't afraid. I was petrified. I pounded those men with my blind hatred for their existence. Nothing could contain the rage that I allowed to course through my veins. I didn't want to stop myself. If Wilfred hadn't pulled me off that man, I would have killed him."

"What you did was brave," Blake insisted.

"It was stupid. Don't you see? I was so consumed by my experiences of the past I recklessly placed myself in harm's way to satisfy my need to punish. Wilfred had a gun. I could have had him release another shot in the air to scare them away. It would have been a safer move. Those men could have been armed, shooting me as I ran towards them. I entered into that situation with little care for my own safety or for yours. I was blindly feeding a need. There's nothing brave about what I did. It was irresponsible, careless and, above all, selfish."

Blake thought about this for a while. "How do we move past this?"

I pondered his question. "I feel you would benefit from continuing your sessions with your therapist, particularly because of your feelings of guilt. You'll need to find a path to forgiveness. Embrace the truth. You did the best that you could at the time. You never really know how you're going to react until you're living the moment. That's true for us all."

"What about you?" he asked.

I hesitated. "I need to acknowledge that a very dark side of me exists. I have to walk an inward path to identify the triggers and find a way to disarm or balance them so I don't place others or myself so freely at risk of danger ever again. I'm not afraid of its existence. I'm afraid I won't be able to control it when it surfaces. To me, acceptance is the key to finding where my truth lies in the darkness."

I could hear the music from an ice cream truck approaching.

"Come," I said as I cut across the grass to the footpath.

Blake followed. I took him to the playground where the truck had now parked. There was a queue of excited children. I pulled some money out of my wallet and waved it to get the ice cream man's attention.

"Give them any ice cream they want. My shout, kids."

They screamed with joy and all pushed forward to get their treat. We both watched, drinking in their delight.

I looked across at Blake. "Sometimes, when you're struggling to see kindness, you need to create it to remind yourself it does exist."

A lady walked towards us with her son, pushing him forward. "What do you say?" she encouraged.

In a squeaky little voice, he said, "Thank you."

I crouched down so I was at his eye level. "You are very welcome, little man."

He turned and skipped off to resume playing with his friends.

As I stood up, his mother said, "That was really nice of you."

"My pleasure. It was nice to be able to do it."

She smiled and went back to the playground to watch over her special little guy. I settled the bill after the last child had been served. Then I sent Blake home to get some rest and returned to the office. It had been an emotional day.

***

I realised talking to Blake had helped me clear my thoughts. I knew what I needed to address but was yet to find a way to do it. This would be my focus; I had to find a way to guide myself to the answers.

That night my dreams were flooded with random images. A raven squawked at me while the symbol of Papa Legba emerged from the darkness. The man I had beaten unconscious took form and laughed. Hands beat on a drum. Water bubbled from the earth. An empty boat floated on a calm ocean.

I woke in a sweat.

As a collective, I didn't know what all of the imagery meant, but I understood them individually.

The raven symbolised darkness, but was known to be a guide for wisdom in unveiling secrets. Papa Legba was the gatekeeper of the crossroads between the living and the dead. I wasn't sure what the face of the man I had beaten represented. There had been four men yet his image was the only one present. The drumbeat provided a mechanism to guide me to a hypnotic state.

The water was a channel to cross the planes. The boat I assumed was a symbol of my parents' death at sea.

I lay awake for the rest of the night thinking about these images.

They had to hold a collective meaning.

My mind kept flitting back to the boat. It was clear enough for me to see it in detail. It was empty. The sea was so still. Why did the calmness of the sea irritate me?

***

At the break of day, through some Internet research, I located a woman who was said to be a renowned voodoo practitioner. I briefly spoke to her on the phone, packed an overnight bag and headed to see her in New Orleans.

I arrived at her home. It looked like any other in the district. I'm not sure what I was expecting but felt surprised the house was so vanilla in design. She greeted me at the door and took me to a room at the back of the house. It was filled with candles and there were magic symbols on the floor. The table to my left was cluttered with bottles, feathers and what looked like pages torn from books.

"The knowledge you seek to see will change you forever. The answers we gather are never the ones we intended to find," she warned.

"I've done this before when I was six. My friend Marlee opened the door to the crossroads so that I could see something I needed to know." I took a deep breath as I thought of my parents.

"You travelled the planes as a child?" she questioned.

"Yes, she wanted me to see what she could not speak of."

The lady nodded and looked down for a moment. I knew she recognised it was the message of death. She raised her head and looked at me with softer eyes. "Tell me again what symbols you saw in your vision."

As I told her about them, she walked around the room gathering some items. She handed me a raven's feather then poured water into two bowls and placed them on the floor inside a circle surrounded by symbols.

She stood in front of me and stared into my eyes. "Are you sure you want to do this?"

I stepped into the circle and sat down with my legs crossed. Placing the feather in my hair, I placed my hands into the bowls of water. "I'm sure."

She reached forward and with her thumb she marked a cross on my forehead with a viscous liquid. "This will keep you safe and guide you back."

She switched on a sound system so the room was filled with the rhythmic beat of drums. I closed my eyes and waited.

I felt her breath as she blew powder onto my face and whispered, "See what you need to see."

My face itched from the powder. I could feel the sound of the drums intensify in my mind. The water surrounding my hands started to bubble as the heat rose through my body. I was sinking. The louder the drums beat the deeper I fell. I was falling between space and time with no end in sight.

The raven called and I turned to my left. It was perched on a branch. It looked at me and then ahead, so I turned to follow its gaze. Water glinted in the distance but besides that there was nothing to be seen. I walked across to the raven and held out my hand. It flew down and settled on my arm.

"Show me," I whispered.

The raven glared into my eyes. Lost in the blackness, I felt myself lift from the ground. I was soaring above the ocean, headed out to sea. I could feel the expanse of the raven's wings and the wind underneath my body, carrying me. The boat from my dreams appeared in the distance. As we headed towards it, I noticed the sea was calm. I felt cold as we approached.

We hovered above the boat and I could see three people who looked like they were arguing. My body shivered as I witnessed two tussling before one fell down. The third person tried to escape but was chased. I felt the need to yell but had no voice to command as I watched this person being struck down. The one left standing dragged the bodies to the side and threw them overboard. I was enraged.

The raven resisted my desire to fly down. I wrestled with its will to force it closer to the boat. I had to see, I needed to see. As I soared adjacent, I witnessed the face of the man. He was covered in blood and smiling as he wiped his hands on his shirt. The raven fought against my inclination to attack him. Instead it flew into the ocean and swam to the people who had been thrown overboard. The water was cloudy with the blood that seeped from their bodies. They were lifeless, gently floating in the passive currents.

It was my mum and dad.

I gasped for breath as I heard the beat of the drums. I coughed up water onto the floor and snatched at my throat in an attempt to aid my breathing.

I was soaked with sweat and back in the land of the living.

Shaking my head, I spoke through clenched teeth,

"It was him. He killed my parents. He wanted to charge them more for the boat tour. When they refused, he killed them. They died for nothing." I rocked back and forth as I cried into my hands. I had been denied a life with my parents because of greed.

When I had recovered my composure, I looked across at the voodoo priestess. "Why didn't I see this as a child? In my vision they were covered in seaweed and I couldn't get it off them. The more I tried, the more grew back."

"They were protecting you. You only saw they were dead so you didn't spend your life searching. You weren't shown the whole truth for the same reason. If you had seen what really happened back then you would have spent your life with hatred and revenge in your heart. They loved you and wanted you to live without this."

"Why would they show me now? What good does it do?"

"The man who slayed your parents, do you know him?"

I closed my eyes and took a deep breath. "Yes," I said calmly.

"He has crossed over. Did death come to him because of you?" she asked.

"Yes," I said, knowing that she already knew the answer.

"He was black of heart. Your hatred for him was connected. You may not have known in your mind, but your spirit was in tune. Did you harbour guilt over his death?" She altered her position to gaze into my eyes.

I looked back into hers so she was able to read my truth. "No. I didn't care. I considered his eradication to be a kindness to humanity. My purpose in coming here was to find what drives my anger in order to curb its uncontrollable rule over me."

"Trust that you have your balance. Darkness and light exist in you in equal parts," she said, placing her hand on my arm.

The warmth of her touch made me shiver.

"You wanted to go through the crossroads to see. Now understand this: what you were shown was greater forces in the universe at work. They fuelled your anger. You were the channel used to claim the revenge your parents sought. They are at peace now."

Calmness washed over me as I listened to her message. I could feel the essence of relatable truth in the words she spoke. I wanted to believe my parents were now at peace and able to move on. If I had contributed in some small way to making this happen then I was a willing and grateful vessel at their service. The voodoo priestess was right: I had gone in with questions and walked away with answers that I didn't know I was seeking. Nothing is ever as it seems.

Exposed

That last experience crossing over changed me. I now seemed to see things clearer than I had before. I felt this strange ability to hear people's thoughts, not as a voice, but rather as *knowing* what they were thinking as opposed to what they chose to convey. It was as though my sixth sense had amplified.

Blake had found success through therapy. The glisten in his eye was present once more. It gave me hope that things would return to normal, if not better, for him. He deserved to be surrounded by joy. It was a relief to know his witness of my darkness hadn't deterred him from staying on the team. Our friendship grew stronger from the experience we had shared.

The team was making preparations for New Year's. Solution Manifestation was fast becoming a global presence. The work being undertaken to bring clean water to the world was happening. We were about to complete our one hundredth project and plans were in the pipeline for two hundred more. People from all over the world volunteered to assist at sites. The concept had developed a life of its own.

Michael came into my office with a concerned look on his face.

"What is it?" I asked.

He reached across and placed a paper on my desk. "Page 23. You need to read this."

I skipped to the page and saw an unflattering photo of me. The title in large bold font was "The Secret Millionaire." I read the article in disbelief. This reporter spoke in scathing tones about my hidden wealth, suggesting that Solution Manifestation was a front to fatten my ever growing wallet. It went on and on. I stopped reading halfway through. I had seen enough.

Michael stood waiting.

"Is there anything else?" I asked.

"The phones have been off the hook with media requests. They insist they want access to you."

"Get the list and give it to Blake," I said calmly.

"They won't accept an interview with him. They are all making it very clear that they want to interview you."

I tapped my fingers on the desk while I thought. "Call the reporter who wrote this article and tell her I want to meet her off the record tomorrow. Get the accountants to create a full financial breakdown of the company's finances by the end of the day. Find out from Blake who the most reputable media channel is so we can set up an exclusive interview. I want it to be streamed live. It has to be unaltered so they don't have a chance to misrepresent what I say. Got it?"

"Yep, I'm on it." He walked out the door.

I reached across and opened the newspaper to finish reading the article. As I completed the last paragraph, Blake walked in.

"Hey, sorry. I got here as soon as I heard."

"I guess it had to happen sometime," I said with a smile.

"Is it true?" he asked.

I scrunched my face. "Is what true, exactly?"

"That you're filthy rich," he said cheekily.

"I guess you could you say that. Yes, I have a lot of money."

He walked across and sat in the chair. "Why would you hide it?"

"I didn't hide it. It just wasn't something that I felt compelled to talk about. You're a self-made businessman. You once told me you were rich, right?" I said, looking across at him.

"Yes."

"When you started making some serious money, did you find people treated you differently?"

His bottom lip pursed as he responded, "Yeah, people can be arses. They tried to ride on my coat tails. Some of my closest friends attempted to spend my money for me. We would go out for dinner and they always expected me to pay because I was the man with the fat wallet."

I laughed. "To my mind, nothing good comes from people knowing too much about finances. It becomes something you are defined by and regarded for, yet it's nothing but a piece of plastic that has an exchange value associated with it."

He hesitated before he asked his next question. "How did you acquire your wealth?"

I looked at him for a moment and then stared out the window. "I inherited it from my parents when they died. It was held in an estate until I was twenty-one, and then I was awarded control."

"I'm sorry, Talia. I didn't know about your parents."

"It's OK. How could you know something that I chose never to divulge?" I looked down at the article again.

Blake leant forward. "What are we going to do about this? The media is in frenzy. You know you're going to have to face them. They won't accept a response from me. Not this time."

"I have a plan. I've told Michael to get me an off-the-record catch-up with the reporter who wrote this."

Blake raised an eyebrow and a half-smile spread across his face. "What are you expecting to achieve with that?"

"I want to find out what motivated her to research me and write the story in the first place. Once I understand her original drivers, I'm going to step through the article and get her to explain her thoughts and associated conclusions. She judged me and hung me out to dry without any attempt to validate anything." I had a cheeky grin on my face as I continued. "I expect by the time I'm finished with her she'll accept my invitation to join me in the TV interview we will set up so she can explain her approach and conclusions. I think it's the least she could do."

"I love the way your mind works, genius." He leant back in his chair.

"I'll need you to set up some surveillance cameras in my office tonight. Make them high quality with good sound. If she decides to decline my offer tomorrow then I'll release the tapes to the media and YouTube so the truth can be established. I'll then do the interview on my own to clear the air."

He shook his head as he stood up to leave my office. "Remind me not to get on your bad side."

***

When I left the office that evening there were reporters waiting for me. Flashes from cameras were going off as I raised my hand to block their view. The interest in the story had grown out of proportion. I jumped in the car and drove off without saying a word. Tomorrow would be the day of reckoning.

***

The next day, Michael walked into my office with a woman. "Talia, this is Mila Jones, the reporter who wrote the article on you."

I stood up and shook her hand. "Come and have a seat. Would you like a cup of coffee or tea?"

"Depends, is it bought with charity money or yours?" she said in a sharp tone as she sat down.

I wasn't going to let her bait me. "It's mine."

"I'll have a tea, one sugar, white."

I smiled at Michael. "Can you organise it, please?"

"Sure." He left.

I addressed Mila. "Thanks for coming. I wanted to have a chat with you off the record. Are you still OK with doing that?"

She smiled in a way that made me suspicious. "Sure. I'm here, aren't I?"

"Yes, you are. I want to hear you say the words," I insisted.

She rolled her eyes and shifted her position in her seat. "Anything we say is off the record."

I knew she was lying. Her body language betrayed her.

I clasped my hands together and smiled. "OK, then. Let's get started."

She mistook my words as permission to speak. "You're a thief and the worst kind. You pretend to be charitable, praying on the generosity of people to obtain an obscene amount of wealth for yourself."

I scratched my head, amazed at her accusations. I chose to ignore her slant. "What motivated you to do the article?"

She folded her arms. "I'm assigned to research and report on charities. I was up to 'S' so I was looking at the company and all the people in it."

"Why did your interest fall on me?"

"You were the sole founder of a charity that had a global presence and yet I couldn't find anything about you on social media. No photos, no interviews, nothing. Blake was linked to this place but you were a ghost. I found it suspicious, so I started to dig. That's what a good reporter does," she said, still maintaining a tone that was starting to grate on my nerves.

Michael came in and placed the cup in her hand. Then he turned to me. "Is there anything else you need?"

I smiled at him, knowing that he was worried. "I'm good, buddy. Thanks."

I addressed Mila again. "So you started to dig. What did you find?"

"Did you read the article? I think it's pretty obvious. You're obscenely rich. That money had to come from somewhere. There's no record of you ever holding a job. You just appeared out of nowhere and hid from view. That reeks of corruption from where I sit."

"So what I am hearing you tell me is you somehow managed to find out my bank balance, identified I was in a position of 'obscene' wealth, as you put it, and then leapt to the conclusion that it was obtained through dodgy channels."

"Do you deny it?" She smirked.

"Yes and no. Before I explain my response, I want to know: was there anything else you discovered in your research to validate your scathing accusations on my character?"

She shrugged. "What more do I need? The facts speak for themselves."

"The facts. Your only fact is confirmation I'm wealthy. I have never held a job; that's true enough, and I have never been the spokesperson for Solution Manifestation. Why didn't you offer me a chance to speak with you before you printed the article? Surely due diligence would dictate the need to validate your findings."

"I didn't see a point. You would have lied and it would have given you time to hide the corruption."

I laughed. "I think you might have watched too many movies. I'll explain my 'yes and no' answer now. Yes, I'm well off. Did I obtain it through dodgy means? Absolutely, it was obtained through the dodgiest of means. I acquired my wealth through the death of my parents. I gained control of their estate when I turned twenty-one. The funds keep growing because, outside of some basic living expenses and the money I use to sustain Solution Manifestation, I don't touch it, so it keeps growing. All the costs associated with running the team, this building, the utilities, the advertising are paid for by me with my 'obscene' amounts of money. The front man, Blake, works here for free. He's rich, too, but he didn't seem to get a mention. A hundred percent of the money donated by people is channelled directly to the projects. I make up the deficit if we fall short."

Still sceptical, she asked, "Why would you ask for charity when you could fund it yourself?"

"It's a good question, one that might have been better served being asked before your article was written. I'm a firm believer in the importance of contribution. In order to create awareness and sustain a vested interest, you need to have people care. I wanted to give anyone an opportunity to contribute. It could be in the form of an idea, an inspiring story, a monetary donation or donating their time. Anything they offered through free will would be accepted in good faith for the cause. If you teach people to fish they can feed themselves. That's why we always hire people in the communities we are helping. We want them to feel a sense of pride. It's not just about giving them clean water; it's so much more than that."

"If what you're saying is true then you won't have a problem with handing over your financial breakdown."

I held her gaze. She still insisted on retaining her suspicions.

"I have no interest in providing you with anything. I have an alternative proposal. I've set up a live interview next week on the Hub. I'm going to give their researchers full access to my accountants, my staff, and I'm prepared to foot the cost of sending the researchers to one of the projects if they want to see what we do first hand. What I would like is for you to join me at the live-to-air interview so you get their findings first hand and can respond."

"Why would you want me there? You know I'm not going to hold back."

I shook my head, astounded. "I have nothing to hide. I know they will confirm what I told you today is true. Then you will be faced with the responsibility of explaining to the viewers why you thought it was acceptable to run with a story with no foundation to sustain your accusations. I can then call the paper into question for defamation, given the established irresponsible journalistic technique that they obviously support." I sat back in my chair and smiled.

Her expression changed. She no longer looked smug and confident. "I'd lose my job," she said, her brow creased.

"Yes, you will."

She clasped her hands and leant forward. "I don't know what to say."

"I have an alternative solution for you if you'd like to hear it."

"What is it?" she asked in a small voice.

"You can write another article. It would be an apology for the misrepresentation you made. I don't want it to make any reference to my parents' death, but you can say my wealth has been derived from family money. You have to ensure it is clear to all that the charity is unscathed and all moneys donated are a hundred percent allocated to the cause. Blake will work with you to provide you with the facts you need to get it right this time. I would also like the paper to make a donation to Solution Manifestation in good faith as a token of apology for defaming my character and telling the world that I have money when I spent a lifetime keeping it low key. No thanks to you, I'm now going to be treated differently by people. I won't be able to fly under the radar, which was my right. You stripped me of this with no consideration. Remember that the next time you feel compelled to pass judgement."

She looked down at her feet. "How much are we talking about?"

"In terms of the donation? That's up to the paper to decide. I'm not going to dictate the value. They can come up with a figure and I will accept whatever is provided.

The only condition is that the donation amount is listed as part of the article."

I stood up and crossed to the door. "I think we're done here. Call the office to confirm if the terms are accepted before the end of today. Let me be clear: the offer expires today. If I don't hear from you, tomorrow I'll accept the Hub's offer for an interview. Once I do this, I won't reverse the decision. I'll do the interview with or without you, and then my lawyers, paid by my 'obscene' wealth, will be making a visit to the paper to get the proceedings in place for what I promise will be an expensive payout when they lose. All of which I will donate a hundred percent to the cause. Are we clear?"

She stood up slowly and walked towards me. "Yes. It's clear." She paused just before the doorway. "Talia, for what it's worth: I'm sorry."

I bit my bottom lip. "I bet you are. I'm just not sure whether it's because you have remorse for completely fucking me over or because I turned the tables on you. Apology accepted."

She left without another word.

***

In the afternoon, I asked the team to gather in the conference room, where I played the security tape on the big screen for them. I knew they harboured curiosities about the article and even more about my meeting with Mila. This was the easiest way to address all their unspoken questions regarding my wealth. I left them to look at it while I returned to my office to work. I could hear them laughing and cheering. It was a good outcome, better than I had hoped for considering the attitude she had walked in with.

Some time later, Michael came into my office, beaming with joy. "Mila just called to confirm the paper has accepted your terms. They are drafting some legal papers for you to sign, confirming the donation would remove all obligations so no law suits will be instituted."

"That's fine. Let them know I'm OK with the terms."

"I already accepted," he said, smirking.

"Good job. Thanks, Michael."

He walked across to where I was sitting, leaning in to give me a warm embrace. "I'm sorry about your parents."

"So am I, Michael. So am I."

Blake and the team worked with Mila to provide her with all the facts she needed to write the new article. When it went to print, it caused an outrage. People were annoyed at being misled. This created a new wave of media attention focused on Solution Manifestation, supporting the cause, and assisted in promoting all the great work being done. The donations hit an all time high and the paper issued us a cheque for two hundred and fifty thousand dollars. It was nice to have something good come from me being thrust into the public eye.

Sands of Time

New Year's Eve was almost upon us. I had made arrangements for a large celebration to take place for the team. Exhausted, I decided to head home to Australia to be around my creature comforts and away from the watchful eyes of the media. Since the release of the original article, I had been constantly harassed for interviews. I even made it into the top one hundred most available bachelorettes. I cringed at the attention. I left in the hope that the interest would die down in my absence.

***

Brad was at the airport to pick me up. It was nice to see a familiar face in the sea of strangers all waiting for their loved ones to come out of the customs' doors. He greeted me with a warm cuddle, exuding excitement at the thought that we would all be together for New Year. I hadn't joined them in the celebrations in years.

"How was the flight?"

"It was good. I slept for most of the way so it went fast, considering the distance."

I watched him as he drove, smiling like a fool.

He had a natural joy about him that was contagious.

"So, how does it feel to be in the public eye?" he said with a wink.

"It sucks the fat one. What you think?" I laughed.

"I have to say, when I read the first article I felt sorry for the reporter. She didn't know what she had just unleashed," said Brad.

"Hmm, she was a piece of work. It all got straightened in the end and it helped the cause in a positive way. I guess something good came out of it. I can't complain."

"Congratulations on being number fifty-six on the most eligible bachelorette most wanted list." He laughed as I covered my face.

"Urgh, I know. What a nightmare. The poor office girls have been swamped with people calling to ask me on dates. I've had fan mail; some of the stuff they wrote just threw me. There's a lot of lonely hearts out there." I shook my head and looked out of the window.

"Well, you're quite the catch and you do make it impossible to let anyone love you. Except for me, of course," he said smugly.

"Yep, I'm fussy."

His voice changed when he asked the next question. "Do you think you will ever allow yourself to fall in love?"

I thought about this for a while. My thumb gravitated to my mouth so I could chew on the edge of my nail. I didn't know how to answer the question. Did I believe it was possible or whether it was going to happen for me?

"I don't know, Brad. I'd like to think so but I really don't know."

Brad reached across and held my hand in his. We sat in silence for the rest of the journey, listening to the music on the radio.

***

Brad dropped me off at my house so that I had time to settle in before I caught up with the others. When I walked inside, there was a beautiful smell of incense burning, candles were lit and the loveliest bunch of orange gerberas was on the dining room table.

The note read: *Welcome home, love Suzanna and Brad.*

It was a beautiful sentiment.

I dropped my bags in my bedroom and then lay down on the couch to relax. I closed my eyes and drifted off to sleep.

An image of a man appeared. I couldn't see his face. He walked across to where I lay and sat beside me. I could feel his warmth as he leant forward. He kissed me gently on the lips as he ran his hand down my arm to grab my hand. His touch was electric. I could feel my body respond to him and he felt it too.

"Who are you?" I whispered.

"Shhhhh," he responded as he kissed me again. This time his intensity increased. He lingered over my face as he kissed my eyelids, cheeks, chin, and headed towards my neck.

His hands unbuttoned my shirt to expose my torso. I could hear my breathing shift as he ran his fingers on the outline of my bra. The sensation tingled through my body as I found myself arching my back to greet his touch. I knew it was a dream but he felt real pushing against me. He ran his hands down the length of my leg and up, resting his hand on my stomach.

"That's enough," he said and disappeared.

I woke and looked around my empty room. I stumbled to prop myself up while checking to see if my shirt was unbuttoned. It wasn't. I could have sworn he was there. I had never felt the presence of someone in a dream state so clearly before. I couldn't see his face but I smelt his scent. There was something amazing about his command over me. My body wanted to yield to his touch, he was so confident. The only conclusion I came to was that I probably needed to get laid. It had been a while.

***

Brad came over to pick me up while I was in the middle of getting ready. I had taken my time in the shower so I was running late. I opted to leave my hair wet. I towel-dried it, slapped in some product and we were out the door. I was looking forward to seeing the kids.

As we drove up Ruth's driveway, the little munchkins came out towards the car, screaming, "Talia! Talia!"

I couldn't help but smile like a fool at them. They had grown like weeds. Had I really been gone that long?

I knelt and they ran into my arms in a bunch and knocked me over. I laughed as they clambered across one another to get closer to me.

"Come on, guys. Get off Aunty Talia," said Brad, making no attempt to peel them off me.

I could see he was enjoying watching the onslaught of love oozing from these crazy critters. All I could do was laugh. Eventually Brad intervened, picking them up by their pants and moving them to the side. When I stood up my back was covered in dirt. I patted myself down.

"Here, you missed a bit." Brad slapped me on the arse – hard.

I leapt forward and rubbed my cheek. "Gee, thanks. All better?"

"Yes, I feel much better," he said with a roaring laugh. He was still as cheeky as ever.

***

Inside, the procession of kisses and cuddles continued until we sat at the table for dinner.

Ruth, Samantha and Suzanna had cooked an elaborate meal of roast lamb, vegetables and mashed potatoes. The smell of the eucalyptus trees outside wafted throughout the house, reminding me I was home. I was grateful to be with them and to know they held so much love for me. I felt nostalgic as I watched them pass the plates and eat their food. I was indeed blessed.

"Thanks for creating the special touches in the house, Suzanna. It was a nice surprise to come home to. The flowers in particular are lovely."

"Actually, Brad bought the flowers and incense and lit the candles. I cleaned the place for you so you could relax when you got home. It was my way of giving thanks for letting us live there while we built our place." She smiled.

Brad kicked me under the table and I chose to ignore him.

"That's right. How does it feel to be in your own home finally?" I asked.

Suzanna smiled, knowing I was intentionally ignoring Brad and it was obviously irritating him. "It's fantastic. We've been in there three months now. I'm still changing the furniture around. It's not quite right yet but I'm getting there. You should come over tomorrow to have a look."

"I'd love to."

"Talia, I'm sorry about those awful things they wrote in the paper about you," said Ruth.

"Don't be. It's all sorted; nothing to worry about. I promise." I reached across and touched her arm.

"So what's next in the world of Talia?" asked Shane.

"I'm not sure. I plan to have no plan for now. I just want to spend some time at home and see what I feel like doing next."

"What about the work you were doing with that water charity thing?" he continued.

"All the hard work is done. The team know what they're doing. I don't need to be there. I can log in remotely and execute anything from the comfort of my lounge," I said.

"Impressive. Technology has really advanced," Shane said mid-chew.

Brad continued to randomly kick me under the table. I looked at my food and tried my best to ignore him. Everyone noticed he was getting annoyed and they were quietly amused at the two of us at it again. I was his play toy and he clearly didn't like to share.

***

After dinner I read a bedtime story to the kids. It wasn't surprising that I was lumped with more of the Dr Suess books. It was only in the sweet presence of the children that I realised how much I had missed them. They were little bundles of energy and delight. As a special treat I read them three books. Mia was the only one who stayed awake until the end. I finished tucking them in and left the room.

Everyone had settled in for the night. Country folk went to bed early and rose at the crack of dawn. Brad was in the lounge, sitting by the unlit fire, waiting for me. He had opened a bottle of red and passed me the glass he had already poured.

"Thanks." I sat in the chair opposite him.

He had a smirk on his face as he sipped his wine, watching me stare into the flames of a candle on the mantle.

"What?" I said, knowing he had something up his sleeve.

"If you're going to be around for a while, I could introduce you to some of my single mates."

"Ew! No, thanks."

"Why not? There's one in particular I think would be right up your alley."

"How would you know what kind of guy I'd be into?" I said, now glaring at him.

"I'm not going to bother answering that. Anyway, we've organised for him to come to dinner at our house tomorrow night so you can meet him. He's busting to meet you."

"No! Are you kidding me? I'm not going on a blind date. No way in hell." I returned my gaze to the candle flame. *What was he thinking?*

"Don't be like that. It'll be fun. Who knows? You might actually like him," he persisted.

"Yeah, a barrel of laughs, I'm sure."

"So it's settled. Tomorrow night I'II pick you up from your house at 5 pm so it gives me a chance to show you around before dinner."

"Whatever." I knew he wasn't going to let it go.

***

Ruth and Shane were keeping the kids so the adults could have a free night, so Suzanna and Brad dropped me off at my home and then headed to theirs.

When I entered my door, I could smell the essence of the strange man who had invaded my dream. *Who are you?* I thought to myself.

That night I slept as soundly as a baby. The jet-lag had caught up with me.

***

In the morning, I lay in bed and thought about my strange sensual visitor. I could no longer feel his presence but didn't feel alone either. There was a comfort in knowing he was near. Perhaps something had attached to me when I travelled through the crossroads. There was always that risk when opening doors to other planes.

***

In the afternoon, still in my pajamas, I heard a car roll up. Brad came in, took one look at me, and laughed.

"That's a strange choice of attire for dinner," he said, raising an eyebrow.

"You're early."

"It's five in the afternoon. You're late." He kissed me on the cheek. "Get dressed."

I showered and changed while he waited. I had completely forgotten about the dinner, too busy enjoying my own space.

***

When we arrived at their house, Suzanna was talking to a bloke. He was wearing tight jeans and a white T-shirt with 'Metallica' written across his chest. I glanced at Brad, who was beaming. I took a breath and together we walked towards them.

"Luke, this is Talia. Talia, Luke," Brad said melodically.

I put my hand out to shake Luke's hand. He took it and reached in to kiss me on the cheek. "Brad didn't do you justice when he described you. You're stunning," he said in a tone that oozed like syrup.

"Thanks, Brad didn't describe you at all," I said, cheekily reclaiming my hand.

"I hope you're not disappointed."

Cringing at Brad's obvious delight, I pulled a face at Brad while responding to Luke. "Not at all."

Suzanna clapped her hands in excitement and then gave me a big squeeze. I think both of them were enjoying themselves a little too much at my expense.

"Right, show me around." I walked towards the house, leaving them to follow, knowing they were all probably pulling faces in silence to one another.

What a nightmare.

Brad took Luke and me on a tour while Suzanna went into the kitchen to prepare the starters. I could feel Luke's eyes on me the whole time. I did my best to ignore the fact that I was clearly going to be the centre of attention. This was not my idea of fun.

We settled in the lounge and opened a nice bottle of shiraz.

"Brad tells me you have a business in the US," said Luke in attempt to kick off some idle banter.

"It's a non-profit charity to assist third world countries in establishing the right infrastructure to bring water to their villagers," I said, bored already with the conversation.

"Wow, that's amazing. It must be so rewarding to be part of something like that."

I nodded my head as I took a sip of my wine. "It is."

Brad stood up. "I'm going to see if Suzanna needs help in the kitchen."

"Subtle, Brad," I said as he left the room, laughing. I changed my tone. "Luke, can you do me a favour?"

"Sure, anything," he said.

"Can we skip the small talk? I get Brad has told you a lot about me. I'd rather exchange some funny stories. Let's keep it interesting. Is that cool?"

He looked at me with a wry smile and took an unusually large gulp of his wine. "I can do that."

Just then, Brad and Suzanna brought in the entrées and we moved to the table. Once seated, Suzanna dished up and we all began to eat.

As Brad took his first bite, I said, "So, Luke, what's your take on the herpes commercial that's being aired on the radio and TV?"

Brad choked down his mouthful while Suzanna and Luke laughed. I smiled at Brad and in a condescending tone, said, "Honey, are you OK? You should chew before you swallow."

He kicked me under the table as he drank his wine to wash the rest of his food down.

"Well, that's a conversation starter if ever I've heard one," added Luke.

"Tell me the best story about your childhood. Describe the first thing that springs to mind. Go," I said to Luke.

Without skipping a beat, he gleefully answered, "Picture this. I was thirteen years old. Nicole, the girl I had a crush on, was sitting in the playground eating her lunch. I decided that it was the perfect opportunity to hang out. I bravely walked across and sat beside her. The lunch box on her lap was covered in *Kiss* stickers, so I used that as my entry point. I told her that I really liked *Kiss* too. She seemed excited by this and asked me what my favourite song was. I went down on one knee, banging my head up and down while playing an air guitar and blurting out the words to *My Sharona*. When I looked up, she had a confused expression on her face and told me the *Knack* sang that song. I was so embarrassed I pretended I knew that and it was just a joke and walked off. I vowed never to have a crush on a girl again." Luke raised his glass and we all cheered.

We spent the rest of the evening throwing random questions at one another to find our most amazing life experiences. The night was filled with laughter. It turned out to be a perfect evening. I would never admit to Brad, but Luke was an awesome guy. He was handsome, carried himself well and loved to laugh. He had a lot going for him. I wondered why he was single but chose not to ask.

At the end of dinner we said our goodbyes and upon Luke's insistence he was the one who drove me home. He was the true gentleman. He opened my car door and walked me to the porch.

"I had an amazing night. I haven't thought of those memories and laughed so hard in the longest time." He was sincere.

"I'm glad. I have to say I wasn't keen on coming out tonight but am pleased that I did."

Luke smiled as he kicked the dirt with his left foot. "The night would be perfect for me if I could kiss you goodnight."

"Who am I to stand in the way of perfection?"

He stepped onto the porch, gently placing his hands on the sides of my face, and leant down to place his soft lips on mine. As he lifted his head to straighten up, he smiled. "Perfect."

"Night, Luke." I turned and walked inside.

***

The next day Brad was at my door at the crack of dawn. He had brought me some breakfast and freshly squeezed juice. As he placed a spread of scrambled and soft poached eggs, sautéed mushrooms, spinach, halved cherry tomatoes and fresh slices of avocado on the table, I went to brush my teeth.

When I returned, I looked at the spread that was laid out. "Did you think there were more people here or are you expecting guests?"

He laughed as he popped a cherry tomato into his mouth. "I was hedging my bets."

"Right, so it didn't occur to you he might be here and you could be walking in on us having a little morning delight? Hmm."

"I know you better than that, Talia. I knew you wouldn't sleep with him last night, but I know you want to," he said teasingly.

"Don't assume, smarty pants. Luke's the type of guy who wants a girlfriend. I can see the longing in his eyes. I'm not exactly the right fit." I sat down to pick at the spread.

"You kissed him," said Brad, also taking a seat.

"That's an assumption on your part." I didn't want to admit to it.

"He sent me a text on his way home so I know you kissed him." He laughed.

I focused on eating my breakfast.

"Admit, you liked him," he continued.

"He's a nice guy. Luke was sweet so when he asked for a kiss I allowed it to happen. It was for him, not me: he requested it as an end to his perfect night."

Ignoring what I had just said, he continued on his tangent. "I told you I knew your type." He smugly leaned back in his chair and patted his stomach.

"You know nothing. I don't even know what my type is, so how could you?"

"I just know. You may not want to admit it, but I think I know you better than you know yourself." Brad flicked a piece of my hair into my face to get me to look at him.

"Really, is that so? What am I thinking right now?" I shifted my chair away from him.

"You're thinking that I'm a genius and you can't stand that I'm always right about you."

I picked up a spoon full of wet egg and flicked it at his head. "Wrong. I'm thinking food-fight." I grabbed anything I could and threw it at him.

He collected some of the egg-goo running down his cheek and placed it in his mouth. "Hmm, delicious."

Quick as a whip, he plunged forward to grab me. I leapt from my chair and ran squealing like a child, knowing there would be consequences for my actions. I glanced back. His hands were full of breakfast goo. I ran into the bathroom, slamming the door as he thundered to a halt against it.

"Talia, come out. It's OK. I won't do anything," he said in his sweetest voice.

"Like fuck you won't, Egbert. I'm not coming out until you leave," I said, laughing hysterically.

He used all his force to reef the door open as I screamed through my laughter, trying to stop his entry. He was far more determined than I was and I was also weakened by my joy. He composed himself when he got access, slowly walking towards me with food dripping onto the floor.

"You started this, Talia. It's only reasonable to accept that I'm going to end it," he said with a wicked look in his eye.

As he drew closer, I reached for his hands, attempting to wipe them on his clothes. He twisted around so my grip was loosened and slapped his hands onto my face until I too was covered.

I kept laughing; it was all too funny. "Now we're even."

He shook his head. "Not even; not yet, young lady." He picked me up and swung me over his shoulder.

I slapped him on the arse, insisting he put me down as he marched across to the shower and dowsed us in water. The mountain-fresh ice-cold water gushed from the showerhead. My body was freezing but I couldn't stop laughing at our childish antics.

Still dripping wet, we cleaned up the mess we had made while I maintained a watchful eye on him. There was the constant loom of threat in his glances that indicated he still felt obliged to pay me back for my unpredictable outburst. I smiled like a fool. It was so much fun having him around. Brad had always been one of the greatest gifts in my life.

When we were done, I walked Brad to the door.

He turned and looked at me. "You are so beautiful when you smile," he said, before walking out.

***

The rest of the day was mine to play. I took a walk around the property and sorted some things in the stables. They were empty, lacking horses, I thought.

"Hi, Talia." I jumped as I heard the voice.

"Shane, you scared me. G'day. What brings you to this neck of the woods?"

"Sorry, I didn't mean to startle you. I thought I would swing past on my way to town to see if you needed anything?" he said.

"No, I'm good. I was just pottering trying to reacquaint myself with this place. Do you want a cuppa?" I asked.

"No, I just had one. Let me know if you want a hand fixing anything. Tommy, Brad and I can come around to help you."

"OK, I'll see," I said.

"I'll be off then. You're still coming to our house for New Year's tomorrow, aren't you?"

"Yep, I'll be there with bells on."

"It's good to have you home, Talia."

"Thanks. It's good to be back."

Shane got into his car and left. He was such a lovely fellow.

I stayed in the stables to organise things until well into the evening. It was only the rumbling of my stomach that drove me to stop. I went inside and whipped up a serve of rice and steamed veggies for dinner. I had a quick shower to remove the coating of dust on my body then snuggled on the couch to read a book. It was so nice not to have anything else to think about. Solution Manifestation was closed for the festive season so there was no need for me to switch on a computer. I felt free.

***

Startled, I woke to the sound of my mobile ringing. I had drifted off to sleep in the midst of reading. I fumbled to take the call.

"Hello," I said in a raspy voice.

"Sorry. Did I wake you?"

"No. Yeah, kinda. I just had a nanna nap."

"It's Luke. Brad gave me your number. I hope you don't mind."

"No, it's fine. How are things?"

"I'm good. Actually, I'm distracted. I can't seem to get you out of my mind," he said in a chirpy tone.

"You should see a doctor about that before it gets any worse," I said with a chuckle.

"Brad warned me that you were unlikely to give much away."

"What else did he tell you?"

"Mostly that you keep your cards close. You don't allow yourself to fall in love easily. That you're not likely to ever settle down in the conventional sense of marriage, children."

"You know all this and you're still calling me. Why?" I tried to make light of the conversation.

Luke cleared his throat. "I like you. I want to get to know you, regardless of the outcome. No regrets."

"I'm not sure what to say."

"I just want to spend some time with you. We can see where it goes from there, OK?"

"No expectations?" I questioned.

"Promise. None. There may be hope, desire, a secret pact made with the devil in exchange for another kiss but definitely no expectations." He laughed.

"Are you coming to the Parker New Year's celebration tomorrow night?" I asked.

In a cheeky tone, he responded, "I am if you're inviting me."

"I am. Catch you tomorrow then."

"Do you need a lift?" he asked.

"Nope, I'll find my own way. Thanks for the offer. Have a good night."

"Night, Talia." He hung up the phone.

I had a shower to warm my skin, slipped into my pajamas and hopped into the comfort of my bed, quickly drifting off into the space of dreams.

I could hear the echoes of children's laughter. My body responded with goose bumps as I identified with the familiarity in their high-pitched voices. They spoke to one another in a whisper; their purity of joy warmed me like a blanket. I couldn't see them clearly, just their little outlines. I didn't know who they were, but I was certain that they cared for each other very much.

***

The morning light shone on my face, greeting me with its gentle rays. I squinted one eye while half-opening the other in an attempt to find my phone to identify the time. In a blur I could just read 7:30 am. I placed the phone back on the bedside table, turned onto my side and slapped a pillow over my head to block out the light. I wanted to sleep.

I could feel his body press against my torso as he sat on the edge of the bed. I twisted my upper body to look at him. I still couldn't see his face yet he radiated a smile that warmed my core. Reaching across without a word exchanged, I placed my arms on his shoulders and guided his body to fall across mine so we were now lying on our sides facing each other. He gently removed a strand of my hair from my cheek and tucked it behind my ear. I ran the fingers of my right hand up and down his left arm.

He put his hand into mine then lifted it to his face, kissing my palm before placing it on his heart. I smiled as I felt the rhythmic beat. Leaning in, he kissed me with knowing skill. My lips surrendered to his playful tongue. I pushed into the kiss as he pulled back. I could feel he enjoyed the upper hand. I wanted him. My body responded to his touch in waves of electric pulses that I had never experienced before.

***

I woke suddenly to the sound of a knock at the door. Propping myself up, I shook my head and rubbed my eyes. It was a dream, an intensely life-like dream.

A voice called out. "Talia."

"Coming," I said, fumbling out of my bed.

Suzanna was in the lounge room picking the dead flowers from the bunch they had bought me as a home-coming gift.

"Morning," I said, running my fingers through my tangled hair.

"It's almost afternoon, sleepyhead," she said, looking at my pajamas.

"Give me a minute. I'll have a quick shower. Make yourself a cuppa. I'll be back in a jiffy."

She walked into the kitchen as I left the room to shower and dress.

Washing my hair in the shower, I thought about my strange dream buddy. When he was present I could feel the warmth of his touch, the velvet of his tongue, the beating of his heart pulsating through his skin, yet it was a dream. How could something so fantastic not exist? I wanted him to be real.

Fully dressed, complete with wet, dishevelled hair, I entered the lounge again.

"What are the plans?" I asked.

"I thought we could spend some time together, perhaps start with getting some lunch?"

Reaching for my purse and the keys to lock up the house, I said, "Great, I'm starved."

***

Suzanna drove to the local Chinese restaurant. It was surprisingly full. We waited to be seated and I could feel the waitress was under pressure.

"I'm not sure she's ever had to work this hard before," I said in a whisper to Suzanna.

"It looks like most of the people in town have decided not to cook today," she replied.

We placed our order and helped ourselves to the Chinese tea on the communal table.

"You seem preoccupied, Talia. What are you thinking about?" asked Suzanna.

A wicked smile landscaped my face as I imparted my cryptic thought. "Do you think someone could fall pregnant from a wet dream?"

Suzanna squealed with laughter and covered her mouth with her hand. "Gosh, I hope not."

We chuckled as I played with my linen napkin on the table.

"Tell me really. What's on your mind?"

"I've been having this dream-state experience about a guy with no face. He seems familiar when I touch him. It's like my body knows him but I can't seem to make a conscious connection. It feels so real. I'm starting to think the message is: the man of my dreams only exists in my dreams."

Suzanna leaned in. "Do you think it might be Luke?"

"God, no. This guy is something else. He is confident, knows what he wants and doesn't hesitate to show it. He's muscular in build but very lean. I'm clueless about who he is or whether he actually exists. I just know I want him to."

Suzanna squeezed my hand.

"This must sound crazy. I feel stupid even talking about it; actually, I'm not sure why I even told you. I can't seem to get him out of my head. So there you go. Now you know more than you want to," I said with a smile.

"I'm glad you told me. I wish I had dreams with such an impact. I might sleep in all morning too." She winked.

"Ha, ha. Yes. Well, him appearing this morning was a happy accident that you interrupted, I might add."

"Well, thank the stars. Who knows? You might have fallen pregnant."

We laughed.

The food arrived at the table. The smells from the kitchen had stimulated my gastric juices. We tucked into our meal and bantered about the kids, love, and travel, among other things. That day I didn't seem to mind sharing my thoughts and Suzanna managed to get a decent glimpse behind the veil of mystery.

On our way out after paying the bill, we were each given a fortune cookie.

I looked at the cashier and said in a whimsical voice, "This will be a sign that guides me to love."

She pointed to the board behind her. It had three different fortune cookie sayings pinned up. "I hope not, because these are the only three messages they contain."

A calm sea will not make a good sailor.
You will find a bushel of money.
Ignorance never settles a question.

We cracked open our fortune cookies.

Suzanna's read: *A calm sea will not make a good sailor,* while my message was: *Follow your dreams; they know the way.* A shiver ran up my spine as I read the words again.

Suzanna leaned over my shoulder. "Well, which one did you get? Are you about to get a bushel of money? Hey, that's not on the board."

The cashier walked around her little podium and looked at the message. "Huh, never had that one before."

"I guess there's a first time for everything," I said as I ushered Suzanna to the door.

We headed to the grocer for some items for the New Year's party. As we walked down the aisles I could see the cogs churning in Suzanna's mind. She was busting to make a connection between the message on my fortune cookie and my mystery dream man.

I startled as she spun round to face me, which meant she was now walking backwards down the aisle. "Do you think it's a sign? Will your dreams guide you to him?"

"Maybe. Stranger things have happened."

She clapped her hands. "This is so exciting. How romantic."

I pulled my hair across my face, cringing. "Ahhh, why did I tell you?"

She flicked my hair away so she could look into my eyes. "Because I'm your favourite sister-in-law."

"Yes, true. My only sister-in-law, but a favourite nonetheless."

Not discouraged by my comment, Suzanna put her arm in mine and we continued shopping while she beamed with delight.

***

When we arrived at Ruth and Shane's, I looked across at Suzanna before we walked in. "This is our secret. No one gets to know this. OK?"

"I promise I won't say a word, but you know Brad will sense something is up," she said, smirking.

"I think our chances would improve if you changed that expression on your face," I said, knowing she wouldn't be able to contain herself.

She covered her face with her hands, then removed them, revealing a cross-eyed fish-lipped expression.

"Oh, yeah, thanks. That will have them fooled." I nudged past her to walk in the door.

"We come bearing gifts," I said, my arms full of groceries.

"Hello, my sweethearts." Ruth walked towards us with open arms.

She kissed us both and then helped fetch the rest of the supplies from the car.

When we were settled inside to unpack the goods, I noticed Ruth kept looking at Suzanna and eventually touched Suzanna's face. "You're positively glowing."

"Yes, she's been radiating all day. Must be my presence," I said to divert Ruth's attention.

Ruth and Suzanna both laughed and continued unpacking.

***

By evening, everything was set for the family New Year celebration. It wasn't long before the house was filled with the sound of overly stimulated children. Brad and Tommy brought in the alcohol, while Shane manned the barbecue with Sammy and her husband James.

"Where's Lisa?" I asked Tommy.

"She's on her way."

"Let's get this party started." I grabbed the champagne flutes and placed them in front of Brad, who was holding a bottle of bubbly.

The cork popped and we cheered. Once the drinks were poured and we'd clinked glasses, Ruth took some drinks out to Shane and the others while I went out to play with the kids to exhaust some of their energy. It was going to be a long night and I wanted the distraction. Inside, the others set the table in preparation for the feast.

Lisa arrived with Luke soon after.

"You made it. Thanks for coming," I said to Luke, who eagerly stepped into my personal space.

In a sultry voice, he responded, "Thanks for inviting me."

I stepped back to reclaim my position. "You're welcome. Go inside and get yourself a drink."

He hesitated before doing as I suggested. I suspected he wanted me to kiss him hello, but I didn't feel the need so I honoured my desire not to. My head was in another space, chasing ghosts, as it were. The thought of Luke in a romantic sense no longer felt like an option. I couldn't see the point in starting something I would never finish. He deserved better.

Once Shane had cooked the meat, the food was placed in the centre of the table and everyone got seated. Sitting back in my chair, I soaked up the atmosphere. I was always so grateful to be welcomed into their lives and made to feel like I was one of them. In this moment my intensity of love for these people flowed through my core.

Brad looked at me smiling. "Eat, Talia." He leant across and started serving me some grub.

The banter flowed easily while we drank and ate. Everyone's spirits were high yet my mind kept drifting to the mystery man without a face. My curiosity was growing and I knew that it would need to be sated somehow.

Luke tried his best to find time alone with me. Thankfully, the kids were more demanding than he was so they won my full attention. We sang songs, played hide-and-seek and, as part of the grand finale, we roasted marshmallows on the remaining embers in the barbecue while I told them fantastical stories that crept into my mind.

Just before the stroke of midnight, we began the countdown outside so the kids could pop some streamers.

"Happy New Year!" they all screamed, hands waving in the air, while streamers flew in random directions.

We exchanged cuddles and well wishes before I took on the duty of putting the kids to bed. I tucked them in and read them a story while they quietly listened. When I left the room, Luke was in the kitchen putting his glass in the sink.

"Hey, you've finished drinking?" I asked.

"Yeah, I thought I might head off. Do you want a lift home?"

"No, I might crash here tonight, but thanks," I said.

I could see he was disappointed that he wasn't going to have an opportunity to spend any one-on-one time with me. I suspected the evening hadn't gone as he had planned.

"OK. Well, I guess I'll be off."

I kissed him on the cheek. "Thanks for coming."

He looked at me, nodded and left.

Normally I would have walked him to his car but felt it was easier if I stayed behind. It wasn't my intention to mislead him. I never should have kissed him. I knew that now.

Brad came inside looking for me. "Hey, is everything alright?"

"It's perfect. Why?"

"Luke just left."

"I know. I said goodbye."

"So that's it? You kiss the guy and then nothing?"

"He's a lovely guy, Brad, but I'm just not into him. I'd rather not start something I have no intention of finishing. That would be cruel."

Brad walked across and put me in his arms. "I just want you to be happy. You can't stay alone forever."

"I don't plan to but I'm not going to date someone for the sake of it."

I knew Brad felt responsible for the absence of love in my life. The truth was I wasn't really sure Brad would have been enough for me either. I loved him. I had an amazing connection with him, but I yearned for something I was yet to discover. I wanted lightning to strike.

Join Up

I placed the fortune cookie message on my fridge as a reminder. I found myself daydreaming about the ideals I would like a partner to have. All of my desires were influenced by the attributes I felt existed in my mystery ghost. At night I wished he would visit. I had so many unanswered questions. I yearned to know his name, where he lived, who he was and, most importantly, why he had such an amazing effect on me.

I could hear my mobile ringing. I picked up the phone and saw it was a blocked number. I hesitated at first then chose to answer.

"Hello."

"Hi, Talia. It's Sebastian."

"Oh, g'day. What's up?"

"Nothing. I haven't heard from you in a while and thought I would give you a call."

I knew he had an agenda. "OK. How are things in your world?"

"I got married, not that you probably want to hear it," he said abruptly.

"Congratulations. Who's the lucky lady?" I said,

ignoring his snipe.

"You know who," he said.

"Ah, OK. At least the cheating ended in something good for you. I'm glad. I assume everything else is well. How is your health?"

"Yeah, it's stable. Talia, can I ask you something?"

Here we go. "Shoot. What's on your mind?"

"Why didn't you tell me you were rich?"

I paused, closing my eyes, knowing precisely why he had called out of the blue. "You read the article."

"Yep. I was really hurt to know you didn't trust me enough after all those years to tell me."

"I didn't think it warranted discussing. In fact, it's still not up for discussion. Let's change the topic," I said, feeling annoyed.

"Well, technically we were in a de facto relationship. We were together for over five years."

"Are you fucking kidding me right now? Seriously. You chose to grow a pair for this?" My blood was starting to boil. That motherfucker was fishing for financial gain.

"I'm just saying that legally –"

"STOP. Seriously, STOP. I gave you more of me than I have ever offered another and now this. I'm going to pretend this call never happened. Don't push me or you will see a side of me you will regret for the rest of what will be your shortened days. Are we clear?"

"I don't want to fight. I just thought … I mean there's enough to go around –"

"See ya, Seb. Don't call me again. Ever. I'm done."

I hung up the phone and threw it across the room. My mind was clouded with fury at his audacity. Imagine him laying false claim on my parents' money! What an arse. All those years, the time spent with him, had only resulted in betrayal. I could see now he was clearly a user. It saddened me to my core to know someone I had chosen to love would be so unworthy of everything I had given him. How could I get it so wrong?

***

When I told Brad about the call, he was infuriated. It took all my strength to hold him back from jumping into his car. He wanted to confront Sebastian and punch him in the nose. I agreed with the sentiment but Seb wasn't worth the hassle. This was just another universal reminder of the ugly side of greed.

***

Luke eventually came around to the idea of hanging with me as a friend. He spent countless days on the farm helping me potter, getting things back into order. I enjoyed his company. I could see there was always an underlying hope in his demeanour but I held steadfast to my decision not to cross a line. He was not the one for me.

The one thing I consistently felt was absent on the farm was horses. I wanted to get some but didn't want to be bound by responsibility. Thinking outside the square, I opted to advertise for a farm hand cum property manager who could maintain all I had created in my absence. The stable quarters needed to be cleaned up, but they would provide a nice space for the right person to live in.

Several applicants came through but it was Ashley who I decided to hire. She was a thirty-year-old single girl who wanted to move away from clerical work to explore other opportunities. I liked her instantly for no apparent reason. She just seemed honest and easygoing.

She laughed at my jokes, which was always going to play in her favour.

Professional painters gave the stable quarters a fresh look. Together, Ashley and I purchased some furniture and she moved in a week later. I was not used to having people in my space but knew we would find our rhythm.

Once Ash had settled in, I set up a routine for her so she could get familiar with the chores she was expected to execute. I had never met anyone who was so clumsy. Every day she bore a new bruise or cut.

One day, while we were working side by side out in the yard, she wiped her brow with her hand and asked, "Is Luke single?"

"I believe he is. Why? Are you interested?" I said with a smile.

"He's cute, but I think he likes you. I'm assuming that's why he keeps coming around."

"Nah, we kissed once but I'm not into him. He's the type of guy who wants a girlfriend and I'm not really interested in playing the role."

"Why not? Don't you want to get married one day?"

"Hmm, I'm not sure. The jury is out on that one. I'm more likely to one-night-stand a guy and if he's any good he gets a three-night pass but that's the extent of my commitment," I said with a laugh.

"Don't you get lonely?"

"Not really. I'm lonelier in the company of the wrong person than I ever would be on my own. I hate feeling the intensity of their love when I'm not responding in kind. It makes them stuck in a space where I'm their unrequited. It's not nice," I said with pursed lips.

"Unrequited?"

"It means to have deep affection for someone who doesn't return the same feelings. I like them but don't love them the way they love me."

"Oh, yeah. That would suck. I've had it happen to me a few times," Ash said.

My curiosity was aroused. "Do tell."

"There was this girl Cynthia. She was my first high school crush. I knew she was into girls but she hadn't come to terms with her sexuality so she kept it hidden. We would experiment from time to time but she maintained her pretence by dating one of the older boys. It was really frustrating."

"So you're gay?"

"No, bisexual. I don't have a preference. I just date who I'm attracted to."

"OK, so what happened with Cynthia?"

"She would ignore me in public, but when she had a chance out of sight of judgemental eyes she would kiss me, hold my hand, you know. I eventually came to terms with the fact that she wasn't going to date me and I was sick of waiting for the scraps of emotion she offered."

"That must have been hard for you," I said, hearing sadness in her voice.

"It was until I met David. He was my first guy. We dated for a while. He became my distraction. He was fun in the sack." She laughed.

"Nice."

***

In the afternoon we headed over to the local sale yards. I wanted to see what horses were up for auction. Watching all the horses in their small pens calling out to each other was sad. They knew something was happening to them. Ash and I walked up and down the auctioneer's platform inspecting the horses. I wasn't sure what I was looking for; I only trusted I would know when I saw it.

We finished inspecting them all.

"Looks like it won't be today," I said to Ash.

"Incoming. Late entry," yelled a man from the back.

I looked across and saw a truck reversing towards the pens. The auction staff unloaded the horses as Ash and I walked over to get a closer look at the new stock. The final horse was tied to the back of the open cattle truck. His back legs were also bound to the sidewalls. It was cruel. I watched as four men untied the ropes and nervously let him loose. The moment the horse felt the pressure released he reefed his head and reared, striking out with his front legs. He was magnificent.

The horse was pushed into a single pen, where he snorted and pawed at the ground. He sneered at anyone who tried to get close to his enclosure. I walked across to him and watched. The liver chestnut gelding was lathered in sweat and was shaking from the adrenalin coursing through his body. The back of his legs had large deep scars. I reached my hand into the yard. He snorted at me and feinted towards my hand to threaten me. I maintain my position and kept still. He stomped his hoof, glaring at me, his ears pinned back.

"He's dangerous, love. Leave this one for the knackery. He's no use to anyone," said the truck driver.

I chose not to acknowledge his words. Instead I opened the pen and walked in.

"Hey, get out of there. He'll kill you. Are you crazy?" yelled a man, running towards the gate.

The horse lunged forward in my direction. I didn't move. His huge body brushed past me as he attempted to attack the man who was now behind the gate. I quietly shifted to one side and continued to watch the horse. He had a crooked blaze and a snippet of white on his front offside leg just above his hoof. He stood approximately fifteen hands high and was solidly built. If I was to take a guess at his breeding I would have said he was a Crabbet Arabian cross Quarter Horse. I could tell from his demeanor he wasn't afraid of me. He was scared of this place.

"You have to get out of the pen," the man insisted.

"Just leave us. It's fine. Anything that happens is my problem not yours. Leave. You're pissing him off," I said through gritted teeth.

"You're a silly girl if you think you can save this one. He's already dead inside."

I rolled my eyes. "Just go," I said, trying not to raise my voice.

The man walked off and left me with him. The auction had started. I stayed in the pen watching the gelding. As he dropped his head and licked his lips I knew he was feeling more comfortable with me. I quietly walked to him, gently placing my hand on his neck. At first he reefed his head up and then settled to accept my touch. I slowly ran my hands along the length of his body. He allowed it.

"I'm going to call you Rebel. You're safe now," I whispered.

As I turned to walk out of the pen, he followed me. His nose nudged my shoulder. I quietly shifted to face him and stroked his neck. "I'll be back."

Rebel was the last horse to be auctioned. I was certain they had done this on purpose in the hope I might not stick around. The only bidder against me was the knackery owner.

He grinned at Rebel as he said, "This is a plump one."

They had it in for this horse. I had no idea of his history but knew the knackery never went over three hundred dollars for their meat supply. When I bid above that, the knackery rep seemed to take it personally and it cost me seven hundred and fifty dollars to buy him that day. It was a record amount for a nag. The reality was I would have paid a thousand dollars if I had to. Rebel was coming home with me.

When the hammer struck and the auctioneer yelled, "Sold," I smiled at the knackery man and the truck driver, who was standing beside him, egging him on.

"You'll be begging me to take him for free. That's if he doesn't kill you first," said the knackery cretin.

I arranged for Rebel to be delivered to my property that afternoon. Ash and I went home to ready his stable.

***

When the truck arrived, I cringed to see he was bound again. I should have known better than to leave his transport to someone else. He was clearly distressed.

I asked the truck driver to drive into an open paddock and we lowered the ramp. I walked onto the back of the truck to release Rebel's head collar and then jumped to the side as he reefed back, clattered down the ramp and then galloped off in fury. He snorted and bucked as he claimed his freedom.

"I think you're crazy, Missy. This one's not worth it," said the truck driver as I paid him.

"You can go now," I said, looking him in the eyes.

He hopped into his truck, shaking his head, and drove away.

Ash walked across to where I was standing. "You sure know how to pick 'em."

"He's broken inside, that's all. He just needs to be loved. There's pain in his eyes. I could see it. Nothing in life holds value for him."

"How are you going to fix him? He seemed pretty pissed," she said.

I turned to Ash and smiled. "Patience and love. That's all it ever takes."

I walked into the paddock and closed the gate behind me, leaving Ash on the other side. Rebel and I had some work to do and it was a journey we needed to take alone. He was in the darkest of places. The only way to reach him would be to gain his trust.

Every day I spent hours in the paddock with Rebel. I would walk towards him and he would run to the spot furthest away from me. I responded by quietly walking back and forth to where he was until he chose to stand still. I never touched him, just stood there watching him graze. He wasn't feeling threatened; he was telling me he wanted to be left alone. I understood his need to defy connection and knew he needed to push past that desire.

***

It took just shy of a month before we had what I saw as our breakthrough. We were doing our usual ritual of me walking into his paddock and him running away. This time when he stood still and allowed me to be in his vicinity I walked up to his side and brushed my body against his, turned and walked away. He chose to follow me. I didn't stop to acknowledge him. I walked to the paddock gate, opened it and turned to replace the latch. He stood there and dropped his head.

"Good boy," I said before leaving to prepare his dinner.

***

I spent my days with Rebel and my evenings working on Solution Manifestation. Any spare time I had was taken up researching horse psychology and getting riding lessons. I needed to brush up on my skills in the saddle if I ever planned to back Rebel. I hadn't bought him expecting to ride him but I could see now it was a possibility. I felt it was important to try, as this would be an ultimate test of our trust.

***

One morning I went out to see my boy. He was in the middle of the paddock grazing. When he heard me he lifted his head and called out then cantered to the gate, bucking. As I entered the paddock he stepped forward, dropping his head and resting it against my torso. I put my hands on his jaw line. I felt overwhelmed with relief; Rebel had allowed his anger to shift; he had finally made his breakthrough. This was his way of expressing thanks. It was an emotional moment, one I was never to forget.

***

Everything seemed to fall into place from that day forward. All his firsts came easily. I was soon able to place a halter on his head, lead him into the stables at night, rug him. I knew he was going to be fine. The connection Rebel and I had in horse terms was called join-up. I felt it was important to extend his trust with others as well to ensure he had a good quality of life. Otherwise we ran the risk of him reverting to his previous behaviours if he fretted at the presence of a farrier or vet.

I hired a local horseman called Joe to assist me in extending Rebel's trust of humans. He had been around horses all his life, transforming it into a career. The techniques he used were part of a growing trend called Natural Horsemanship. The style of handling held many ideas, tools and techniques that provided a kinder way of breaking horses in for riding and management.

In the first few sessions Joe had Rebel in the round yard. It didn't take long for Rebel to yield, responding to Joe's kind demeanour. I was relieved to witness Rebel's connection with another human being. The first time we placed the saddle on his back he bucked freely in an attempt to get it off. Against Joe's wishes, I insisted on being the guinea pig who mounted him. Joe was on the ground with a lead, ready for the worst. Rebel accepted me and stood quietly while I hopped on and off his back.

I beamed with pride on the first day we opened the round pen for Rebel and me to go for a wander around the property. His ears were pricked forward and he had a bounce in his step. He was enjoying himself. Joe rode beside me on his palomino gelding as we quietly explored the edges of my land. It was exhilarating.

At the end of the day Joe stuck around to help me pack the equipment away. I was still smiling from the experience.

"You're happy," he said.

"Of course. He's not fixed but he's on his way now to healing. It's beautiful."

Joe leant against the stable door while I folded the saddle blanket.

"You know people don't pick horses. The horses pick them," he said.

"Really? You think?"

"I know it. You may have been attracted to Rebel

because he was broken but he picked you for the same reason. The journey you took was as much for you as it was for him."

I took a deep breath and released it. "Would you like to stay for dinner?"

"Sure."

Ash was out for the night so it was just Joe and me. He organised the fire and set the table while I boiled some pasta and quickly made a light sauce consisting of tossed fresh tomatoes, avocado, parsley, goat's cheese and homemade pesto.

I raised my glass. "To mutual healing."

Joe took a sip of his wine, watching me. "So you admit you needed healing."

My expression was deadpan. "Doesn't everyone?" I said and I placed the food on the table.

"Sure, but some seem more broken than most."

"Are you suggesting that I'm damaged goods?" I said, half-laughing but feeling a little annoyed.

"Well, you're beautiful, intelligent, kind and fiercely independent. You have everything going for you and yet you choose to live out here alone."

I shook my head at his words. "What's wrong with enjoying solitude?"

"You're more of a hermit." He laughed.

"I like my own company. There's no crime in that."

"Let's face it, Talia. You place more value on your connection with animals than with your own kind."

I picked up my fork and gestured he do the same. The food was going to get cold and I wasn't enjoying the conversation.

I decided to turn the tables. "Tell me, Joe, why aren't you in a relationship?"

"I haven't met the right person. I'm not afraid to be in one," he said, staring at me with a cheeky smile.

I slowly took a mouthful of wine. "Neither am I."

"Oh, I can see that," he said, laughing.

"I'm an open book. You can ask me anything and tonight I will choose to answer. Knock yourself out. Use your best horse psychology."

He rubbed his hands together. "Hmm, let me think. OK. Have you ever been in love?"

"In love? No. I have loved, I have lusted, but not love in my truest definition of the word."

Joe folded his arms and leant back in his chair. "Why do you think that is?"

"I've never met anyone who I could fall in love with. It's that simple."

"No, there has to be more to it. People fall head over heels in love all the time. Why would you be an exception? There has to be a reason."

"I think people use the term too loosely. They foolishly fall in love because they ache to be in that space. I've never felt the need to surrender myself to another in totality. I don't see the point."

He raised an eyebrow. "So you hold back your love?"

"No, there's nothing to hold back. If I honestly feel a desire to fall in love with someone I trust I will. I just haven't met a person who evoked such a depth of emotion in me."

"What about Brad?" he asked.

I shifted in my chair and leant forward. "What about Brad?"

"He told me he was once completely in love with you and you were with him."

"Brad would never say that," I said, surprised.

"He did. A few years back. He was in the pub roaring drunk. I drove him home to his parents because he wasn't in a state to drive. On the way he told me all about you."

I folded my arms. "Brad and I were never together. We were young. Yes, I loved him. I still love him but I never allowed myself to fall in love with him. It wasn't meant to be. There was always something that made us not possible."

"But he could have been the one," he prompted.

"I can't provide you an answer because I'll never know. We've both made our peace with the past and have been blessed to create a beautiful space for one another to share our lives. It's enough for me. He has an amazing life with Suzanna. I'm not sure I could have offered him what he has with her. All is as it should be."

"Do you really believe that?"

"Absolutely. Help me clean the dishes," I said as I rose to my feet.

***

Once the dishes were done we sat in the lounge until we finished the last of the wine. Joe continued his questions on the theme of love and I continued to answer. At the end of the night I walked him to the door.

"You're an interesting person, Talia."

"You ask a lot of questions, Joe," I said, poking his ribs.

"I'll leave you with this one last thought. If I may?"

"Go ahead. You will anyway," I said as I leaned my head on the doorjamb.

"You can save and fix as many broken horses as your heart desires, but you're never going to truly fix what's missing in you until you allow yourself to connect and fall in love."

With these words, he leaned in, kissed me softly on the cheek and left.

***

My dreams were haunted by images of the men in my past. All the broken hearts I had left in my wake presented like an endless war veterans' graveyard. I heard them call my name, "Talia, Talia, come back, Talia" over and over as I tried to get away from their voices. The wind carried their echoes, making me feel replete with the agony of their unfulfilled desires. I felt nothing for them in return. What had I become?

Bloodline

The months melted away as I spent my days on the farm. I purchased a couple of ponies for the kids to ride. They loved being at my house and I appreciated the company. My conversation with Joe had cloaked my mind and I was conscious now of the absence of love more than ever before. I just didn't know what I was supposed to do to fix it. I wasn't prepared to date someone for the sake of it so I felt stuck. A bird trapped in a cage, as it were.

When I walked inside at the end of one particularly long day I saw I had some missed calls from a number I didn't recognise. I listened to the voice mail. It was Marton, the man who oversaw my grandparents' property in Europe. Grandfather was unwell. My heart sank. If Marton was calling then it must be serious. I had to go. I sent a text: *I've got your message; I'm on my way.*

I booked my flights to Hungary online and packed a small case of clothes. In the morning, Ash drove me to the airport.

"You have my number in case you need anything. Here's a card and a pin for all the expenses. Buy what you need for the horses. If you're unsure about anything, call Joe and he can guide you if there are concerns. I've organised for him to come round to check on the horses and get their feet done, so you won't have to worry about it. Never hesitate to call the vet if you think there's something wrong. I sent an email to my accountant last night, so he will organise to pay your wages. Got it?"

"Don't worry, Talia. It's under control," she said, touching my hand.

"OK. Is there anything else you can think of?"

"No, I'm good. Go."

The flight felt like it took forever. I was restless and being confined in the plane wasn't helping. I was tempted to let loose and drink but I knew I had to have my wits about me. I stared at the small screen in front of me, trying to distract my mind from all the thoughts attempting to embed themselves.

"You look nervous, dear. Are you scared of flying?"

I looked across at the woman who was sitting a couple of seats away. The flight wasn't full so I had thankfully scored some space on the cattle train. "No, I'm just in a hurry to be somewhere, that's all," I said with a half-smile.

"Jiggling your leg won't get us there any faster," she said.

I looked down at my manic limb and laughed. "Guess not." I placed my hand on my leg and returned to staring at my TV screen. I felt bad. I hadn't been to see my grandparents in the longest time. My life had taken so many twists and turns since I was last there. Visiting them was never a priority and now time was running out. I should have gone to see them more. My mind was clouded with self disappointment for not actively keeping in touch. They were important to me and I never let them know it. I hoped I wasn't going to be too late.

***

When the plane finally landed, I made arrangements to get my bags post haste and hurried out the door to the driver who was waiting. He took me straight out to the property. Marton and my grandmother greeted me. They both had tears in their eyes as they gave me a warm embrace.

"Welcome home," said Marton.

"How is he?" I said.

"He's not well. The doctors don't think that he will live much longer. They have given him some drugs to help him sleep so he is resting."

I looked at my grandmother and smiled as I placed my hand on her face. "How are you?" I said as Marton translated.

She smiled and nodded her head bravely as tears rolled from her eyes. She was in pain. The love of her life was dying and she had to witness it. The tears in my eyes showed her I too was embraced by sadness. My grandfather may not have been present in my life for long but he was important to me nonetheless.

Marton carried my bags inside and we followed. At the kitchen table was a lady I had never met.

"Hello," I said.

"Talia, this is my wife Elena," said Marton.

When Elena stood I could see she was pregnant. Glowing with a warm smile, she came across to greet me. "Hello, Talia."

I looked at Marton, surprised. "You got married? You're having a baby? Wow, that's fantastic."

"Yes, Elena was working in the local village. We met and fell in love. I tried to reach you to let you know but your office said you were travelling."

"Yes, sorry I never got the message. I would have tried to come if I had known."

"I know." Marton left to place my bags in my room.

My grandmother took my hand and walked me into their bedroom, where my grandfather was sleeping. He was hooked up to an IV and a heart monitor provided the only light in the darkness of the room. It was light outside but the curtains were drawn so he could sleep. I kissed him on his forehead.

"I'm here," I whispered.

We left him to rest. I was introduced to the nurse, who was temporarily living in the guest room. She didn't speak any English but I could see she had a kindness about her. I was glad we could afford the option of not keeping him in the local hospital. If he was to die, let it be in a place of comfort surrounded by the ones he loved.

Marton and I took a walk outside.

"What's wrong with him?" I asked.

"His heart is weak. He had a heart attack a little while ago and he has never been the same. He slips further every day. Last week was the start of the worst of it."

"Why didn't you tell me? I could have come sooner."

"He didn't want me to call you. He said you had enough sadness in your life and he didn't want you to watch this. He insisted and made us all promise."

I nodded my head as the tears streamed down my face. I should have known. I was so preoccupied in my own world; I had lost touch with them.

Marton placed his arms around me. "He will be glad you are here."

"I never should have left you guys for so long. I'm so selfish."

Marton turned to look into my eyes. "You are not

selfish. You are the kindest person I have ever known. This is not your fault. People grow old and they die. Your grandfather is no exception."

"I never had a chance to get to know my parents. I get offered an opportunity to know my grandparents and I let it slip by."

"They know you love them and they love you."

"I hope so," I whispered. "Marton?"

"Yes?"

"Thank you for being here with them. I think you have become the son they lost."

"Yes, and it was you that gave me to them. Remember that. We only found each other because of you." He smiled.

***

Out the back of the farm people were working the land. An ox was being used to plough the ground. I looked at the ornate wagons and the rows of colourful tents. It felt as though I was stepping back in time.

"Are they gypsies?" I asked.

"Yes, the same ones we helped a few years ago. They come back every year and work on the farm with us during the growing season. We feed them, let them sleep on our land and give them a portion of the crops in return for their help."

"Wow, how brilliant."

I recognised one man as we walked towards him to say hello. He was the one who had helped me drag the heavy wheel to the wagon all those years ago.

"Hello," I said, smiling.

His face lit up. "Talia." He embraced me in a bear hug.

I hadn't expected him to remember my name. He was truly glad to see me. It was a nice surprise.

He yelled out to the other gypsies. They dropped their implements and came across to greet me. Some looked familiar; others I had not met before. The group had almost doubled in size and some little rug-rats scampered at my legs for attention. Their presence brought life back into the property. I was so grateful to them for their assistance.

***

In the evening we celebrated our reunion outside beside a roaring fire. The gypsy men played their instruments while the women sang folk songs. I snuck into Grandpa's room, drew the curtains so the moonlight could shine on him and left the window slightly ajar. I wanted him to feel a part of what was taking place. I hoped the sound of the music would distract him from his woes.

***

The nurse called us all into the kitchen in the morning to confirm that he had slipped into a deep coma overnight. He was still breathing but she didn't expect he would ever wake up. I watched as my Grandma burst into tears, holding onto Marton's arms while she wept with deep gasps for air. I knew I had to be strong for them. They needed to be guided so the situation could be managed with dignity.

***

During the next two weeks, I helped my grandma clean him, change the sheets. Marton, Elena and I took it in turns to massage his body and move his limbs to keep his circulation stimulated. The last thing he needed was a pressure sore developing. Grandma started to feel there might be hope when colour returned to his cheeks. I knew better; his breathing was laboured. The crackling on his exhale was a sign that he was developing pneumonia. It wasn't going to be long now.

I spent most of the day at his side telling him stories of my travels, secrets I had never shared. Anything I could think of, I spoke about. I knew he didn't understand English but trusted he could focus on the sound of my voice to know he wasn't alone. It was important to me that he knew I was there and I loved him.

A voice called out, "Talia, come quick."

I jumped to my feet and ran out the door, slipping on a puddle on the kitchen floor.

Elena covered her mouth as she tried not to laugh. I looked down and realised I had just slipped in her birth water. *Yuck!*

"Elena's water has broken. I have to take her now to the hospital," said Marton, leaning in to help me up.

"I'm assuming I'm covered in her birth water." I peeled my wet T-shirt away from my back.

"Yes. Sorry. We have no time to clean up. We must go," said Marton in a panic.

"Take Grandma with you. I'll stay here and watch over Grandpa."

"Are you sure? She wants to come with us but doesn't want to leave you here alone."

"I'm sure. Take her. She needs to feel the joy of a birth, not this. Go."

I watched as they drove away. The gypsy kids chased after the car, screaming and waving with excitement. Life was about to be introduced to the world. Finally, there would be something wonderful to celebrate. We all looked forward to the birth of this child.

I stripped off my clothes and stepped into the shower. Birth water was surprising cold considering it came out of the human body. I welcomed the feel of warm water washing over me as I stood there. I didn't want to move but knew that in summer water needed to be used sparingly to ensure there was enough for the season.

Back in my room, I dried off and put on my pajamas. It was still early in the afternoon but I had no intention of going anywhere. I grabbed a book off the shelf and went into Grandpa's room to read to him. I had run out of things to say so this was the next best thing.

When I finished the last paragraph of the third chapter I watched him lying in his bed, almost lifeless. He was still in a coma and continued to inhale raspy breaths. His face looked paler than usual. I looked at his fingernails; they were a pale grey. He wasn't getting enough oxygen into his body.

I left the room to find some white candles, which I finally located in a bottom drawer in the kitchen. I took the scissors and collected a bunch of the most perfect white roses from the garden. Back in the kitchen, I placed the rose petals in a container, added rainwater and half a jar of honey. I mixed it all together and placed it under Grandpa's bed to align with his solar plexus and laid a washcloth on the bedside table. I lit the candles and placed the remaining roses around the edge of his bed.

Sitting back in my chair, I resumed reading. Midway through the sixth chapter, he started to gasp for air and then rigidly held it before releasing. His face was contorted from what I assumed was pain. I grabbed the washcloth, wet it with rose-water from the cleansing water bowl under the bed and placed it across his brow to cool his fever. The monitor showed he was in distress. He was fighting so hard to breathe.

I didn't want the alarm on the monitor to go off. This was not the time for the nurse to be present. I unplugged the cord and stood by his side. Placing my right hand in his, I squeezed it tightly and I held my head above his while I stroked his forehead with my left hand.

"It's OK, Grandpa, let go," I said over and over as I watched him struggle.

I felt him squeeze my hand as I said, "I love you. *Szeretlek, Nagypapa.*"

The tears streamed down my face as he fought to open his eyes. They were dull and dry from being closed for weeks but he saw me. His face lit up as he mouthed the word, "Talia."

"*Szeretlek, Nagypapa, szeretlek,*" were the only words I managed to say before he closed his eyes.

He drifted off and I could see his body physically shrinking as the life force left his shell.

I stroked his head one last time, closed his eyelids, kissed them and whispered, "Say hello to Mum and Dad for me." I burst into tears as I sat back in the chair and stared at his lifeless body. I felt so blessed he had recognised me and knew I was there for him. It meant the world to me. I couldn't have asked for more.

***

The others didn't come home from the hospital for another four hours. I sat in the dark quietly watching the flicker of the candle flames reflecting on things. When Grandma came to the doorway, she hesitated as she looked at him and then at me. I nodded. Her face contorted as she ran to his side, reefing her body across his torso, wailing as she attempted to lift his shoulders to wake him.

Marton went to console her and I stopped him. "Leave her to grieve." He again tried to get across to console her when she released an almighty scream of anguish. "Don't. She just lost the love of her life. Let her be," I said as I started crying again.

Marton put his arms around me and we squeezed each other tight as we cried.

The nurse entered the room quietly. It was obvious we were mourning his death. She took a quick look at the body and left the room to make a call. One by one the gypsies came into the house to pay their respects while my grandma continued to wail. I went outside and bummed a cigarette. I hadn't smoked since I was last in Paris, but today I wanted one.

Marton came outside and sat beside me on the ground. I had a cigarette in one hand and with my other I was sifting dirt through my fingers.

"Was it a boy?" I asked.

"Yes, he is beautiful," said Marton, filled with sadness.

"Thank you for teaching me how to say 'I love you, grandfather' in Hungarian."

Touching my leg, Marton responded, "He would have heard you say it and been proud."

"He was." Another teardrop flowed down my cheek.

We sat there for a while listening to my grandmother's cries being carried through the darkness in waves. The doctor from the local hospital came to write out the official death warrant. No one questioned why the monitor was turned off. I guess they assumed the nurse had done it. Another van pulled up. It was the men from the funeral parlour. They were set to take the body in preparation for burial.

As I saw them enter the house, I looked at Marton. "Now you can go and console her. This is when it counts."

Marton jumped to his feet and ran inside to support her while she watched random strangers remove her husband's body from their bed. I left them to it and walked around the back of the house to see if the gypsies had left the campfire going. The old gypsy lady who had read my palm years before was sitting on her own. I walked up and touched her shoulder. She looked at me with a smile and gestured for me to sit next to her. It was a balmy evening but still the warmth of the flames flickering on the surface of my skin was welcome. The old lady gently grabbed my hand and held it in hers. I continued to stare at the fire. I needed to get lost in the depths of the flames.

***

"Talia, wake up," said Marton.

I stretched my hand up in the air and lifted my head off the ground. I had fallen asleep in front of the fire. As I sat up I released a big yawn, rubbing my eyes in an attempt to adjust to the light. I could feel the tingling sensation in my right arm as the blood flow was restored. The fire was out and the gypsies were starting to emerge from their tents.

I looked around. "Where's the old woman, the palm reader?"

"She is not with us anymore," said Marton, looking down at the dirt.

"I sat with her last night, just here. She was holding my hand as I stared at the fire. She must have come back," I said, still looking around.

"No, Talia, she died two years ago. She is gone," said Marton.

I looked up at him and instantly knew what he was saying was true. She had passed over. I was unsure why she was sitting beside the fire. Perhaps she just missed the place. Still, she hadn't been surprised to see me and I had felt the warmth of her touch.

Marton extended his hand to help me stand. "Talia, are you OK?"

"Yes, just tired and sad."

"We are all feeling the same. I'm going to go back to see Elena and to talk to the funeral people. Will you stay here with Grandma?"

"Yes, did she get any asleep?"

"The nurse gave her something. She's still sleeping."

"Give Elena a big kiss from me."

"I will," said Marton as he headed off to the car.

***

Inside the house, the gypsy women had taken over. Some were cleaning while the others were in the kitchen preparing a feast. It was their tradition to have a dinner for the dead in celebration of the life that had passed. I noticed the extra-large white candle with three wicks lit on the kitchen windowsill. I had read somewhere a candle is lit for the dead and remains alight until they are buried. The light was set to guide the deceased.

The next three days the house was filled with the buzz of gypsies and local villagers who had come to pay their respects. Grandma mostly sat still at the kitchen table, watching the candle dedicated to her husband's life slowly wane in size. This was the first time in her life she had felt alone. Her childhood sweetheart had passed after sixty-three years of marriage. I could not relate to the gravity of her loss.

On the fourth day the body was returned to the manor to be buried in the cemetery at the back of the house overlooking the orchard. Elena had returned home with a bundle of joy who they had named Fredek after Grandpa. It was an amazing gesture, reconfirming the love they had developed for one another. They were truly a family.

The funeral service was surprisingly quick. Grandma seemed more composed than I had expected. She held Fredek while people took it in turn to speak. Once the coffin was lowered into the grave, most of the crowd headed across in droves to the gypsy wagons, where a fire and feast were being prepared for a final send-off celebration.

It occurred to me I was the last of a bloodline. This was the end of the lineage if I decided not to procreate in my lifetime. For a fleeting moment it felt as though an awakening of responsibility was thrust upon me. I looked at Fredek sleeping in Grandma's arms and couldn't imagine creating such a life. The responsibility was too great. I struggled to believe I would find true love let alone create another human being.

The final celebrations were beautiful to witness. The whole village turned up during the course of the evening to pay their final respects, sharing stories that helped to remind Grandma how many lives she and her blessed husband had touched. Copies of a photo taken by one of the local villagers were given to all who attended. It showed Grandma and Grandpa walking down a cobblestoned path holding hands. Everyone shed a tear looking at the obvious love resonating from this priceless frozen moment. Watching the depth of care people showed for her, I knew she would be OK. Her focus had shifted to baby Fredek now, who was a welcome distraction from the emptiness of her bedroom.

***

A week had passed since the funeral. Everyone had started to readjust to the new rhythm of baby Fredek. It was time for me to leave. I loved being with them but felt lost in their presence. I kept looking at the photo of my grandparents walking down that cobblestoned path, holding hands as they had done since they were in their teens. I stared at this and wondered whether life would afford me the gift of such a union. A need grew within me to find a way to reconnect the floating pieces, to believe there was someone out there looking for me. The next leg of my journey had to be about me choosing to look for him too.

I was ready.

Lucidity

The flight back to Australia seemed to take less time than usual. Ash picked me up from the airport. When we were settled in the car, I noticed she was glowing.

"How's your love life?" I asked, partly laughing.

"Geez, straight to the point."

"I only have one life. No point beating around the bush. Speaking of which, who's beating around yours?" I said, bursting with laughter.

Smiling, Ash shook her head as her face went a lovely shade of crimson. "I think you need to guess."

"Hmm, it's either Luke or Joe or both. Which one is it, you dirty birdy?"

"Joe."

"Joe? Really? So what's he like in the sack? Do you make him wear his hat and boots to bed? Is it serious? Give me all the details. Don't leave anything out."

"Geez, slow down, woman. How many coffees did you drink on the flight? I thought you would be jet-lagged and docile."

"Not a chance. Stop avoiding and start divulging.

I want to know everything." I rubbed my hands together in excitement.

"OK, OK. Joe was coming over to help with the horses. One thing led to another and we kinda hooked up. That's all there is to it."

"Ha! Yeah, like I'm going to let you get off that easy. I haven't had any for a while so I need to live vicariously through you. How did the first kiss happen and who made the move?"

"He did. It happened while we were in the stables. I was prepping the feeds when Joe came up behind me and tapped me on the shoulder. I turned around. Next thing you know, he kissed me."

"So you had no idea he was going to do it?"

"Nope, it was a shock."

"Hmm, kinda romantic when you think about it. It's unlike the anticipated kiss at the end of a first date. He just went with an impulse and took a chance. I like it. What happened next?"

"It was stupid, really. I was still in shock so I blurted out that I had to get the feeds done. He smiled and said, 'See ya tomorrow,' and walked away whistling."

"Ha, ha. Seriously, that's too cute. How long after I was gone did all this take place?"

"Four days, maybe a week."

"Did you know he liked you?" I continued.

"Not really. Mostly I thought he was being polite when he hung around. In hindsight he was giving me signs but I guess I was being a bit of an airhead about it."

"Does this mean you're an item?"

"Yeah, things have shifted along faster than I expected. He's asked me to move in with him."

"Wow, he really digs you."

"I haven't said yes yet. I'm not sure that I want to."

"Talk to me. What's the hesitation?"

"Joe seems so sure of what he wants and I've never been clear on anything. I'm still trying to figure out who I am and what I want to be when I grow up. I've spent my life going with the flow."

"Yep, I get it. You need to tell him how you feel."

"I guess I'm scared if I tell him he might stop seeing me. I like him. I'm not ready to stop."

"Honestly, Ash. Talk to him. He'll understand and if he doesn't then I guess you need to accept the outcome. It's better to be honest and deal with it now."

"I know. I'll talk to him tomorrow when I see him."

"Cool, how good is he in the sack?" I said, laughing once more.

"Actually, he's surprisingly good."

"Why surprisingly? Did you say yes to bedding him expecting that he would be crappy?"

"No, I thought he might be awkward and a little mainstream. He's a meat-and-three-veg type of guy so I thought I might be restricted to missionary and doggy style as my choices."

We both roared with laughter. It had been such a long time since I had lost myself in a hearty laugh. Ash was lovely. I hadn't known her for long but it didn't stop us from becoming fast friends. I enjoyed her relaxed demeanour and kindness of heart. I had trusted her from the moment we met.

***

It was great to be back home. We had arrived just after midnight, which meant I hadn't slept in over thirty-six hours. A quick shower was in order before slipping into my flannel pajamas and heading straight into my spectacular bed. I don't recall spending any time thinking before I fell asleep. I was exhausted.

***

Daylight came quicker than I wanted it to. I placed the pillow over my head to block out the sunlight streaming through the window. It didn't take me long to drift into a deep sleep again. I was grateful that it was a dreamless event. I wanted to have peace from any thoughts. I desired stillness and some time to recoup.

"Talia, wake up."

I slowly opened my eyes to see a blurry version of Ash standing in my room. "What time is it?" I said as I released a big yawn.

"It's 6 pm. The whole day has been and gone again. I was worried when you didn't surface. Aren't you hungry?"

"Nope, just exhausted. Have you spoken to Joe yet?"

"No, not yet. I'm waiting for the right moment."

"Such a brave petal," I said sarcastically.

Ash smiled as she responded, "Yeah, yeah. Whatever. Come on. Get up and I'll make us something to eat."

She looked me up and down as we walked to the kitchen. "Nice PJs."

"I agree; they are rockin'," I said sarcastically. I looked at the fridge. "I think you should open the fridge door so you can be greeted by whatever has been rotting in there for the past few weeks."

"Don't be so sure there's anything rotting," said Ash.

I looked at the smirk on her face and opened the fridge. Inside, much to my surprise, were some fresh herbs and vegetables. I could smell a hint of vanilla and lemon in the air.

"I cleaned out the fridge when I got back from the dropping you off at the airport and bought some groceries yesterday to tide you over until you feel like shopping."

She beamed with pride.

I was impressed by her thoughtfulness. "Did you get me the goat's cheese I like?"

"No, sorry."

"Tsk, epic failure, I'm afraid," I said with a cheeky grin. "Thanks, Ash. It was really nice of you."

"I know," she said as reached in to pull some of the items out.

"Homemade pizza?" I suggested.

"Yum."

I defrosted a pizza base while Ash organised the toppings. It didn't take long to whip up a gourmet delight and have a couple of glasses of red poured for us to enjoy. We exchanged some banter about amusing life experiences. I had really warmed to having Ash in my life.

At the end of the meal we quickly tidied up the dishes and I was off to bed again. I couldn't recall the last time I had been this tired. All I wanted to do was snuggle under my doona and pretend the world didn't exist.

***

I woke to the sound of kookaburras cackling outside my window. There was something in their tone that told me they were in on a joke I was yet to appreciate. Regardless of their seemingly mocking taunts, they made me smile; I was home. I lay listening to them while I adjusted to the idea of moving. My body ached all over. I was either run down or about to come down with something horrible. My mind was foggy and I felt unnaturally exhausted.

The effort to shower and dress was extraordinary. Waves of hot and cold flushed over my body. As I stepped outside to be greeted by the warmth of the sun's rays, I felt dizzy, but I slowly made my way to the stables. I wanted to see Rebel.

"Geez, Talia, you look like crap," said Ash, as I entered the stable yard.

"Morning to you too."

"Seriously, you're pale and you look unstable on your feet. Are you OK?"

"I'm not feeling the best. I'm a little dizzy and I'm finding it hard to breathe."

"Let's get you to a doctor. You need to have this checked out before it gets any worse."

Normally I would have resisted but I had no energy to disagree. "Can you bring Rebel in here? I want to give him a cuddle before we go."

"Sure, he's in the paddock. I'll go grab him. Here, come and sit down." Ash steered me towards the feed room and brought out a chair, which she placed behind me and then guided me into the seat. She touched my forehead with the back of her hand. "Holy crap! You're burning up."

"Rebel," I said.

She looked at me. "OK, pat him and then we're off. I think you need to get to a doctor now."

I closed my eyes and leaned on the feed room wall. "Rebel," I said once again with a smile.

She left and quickly returned with my boy. When he saw me sitting just inside the door, he called out and attempted to break free from the lead. He quickened his pace so Ash was almost jogging beside him. He whickered, thrust his long neck through the doorway and dropped his head into my lap. I stroked his face and breathed in his smell.

"Hey, boy," I whispered as I ran my finger through his coat.

Rebel lifted his head and placed his muzzle on my forehead, inhaling my scent. Without warning, he opened his mouth and started licking me. I laughed then realised he was trying to reduce my fever. My lovely man had detected I wasn't well and this was his attempt to nurture me. Tears welled in my eyes.

"OK, Ash, you win. I don't feel so well. Let's go to the doctor's."

"Come on, Rebel," she said as she gently tugged on his headstall.

Rebel had other plans. He stomped his hoof and reefed his head back into position so he could resume licking. I raised my hands and placed them on his cheeks as I slowly stood up.

"It's OK, boy. Come on." I took the lead rope and slowly walked towards his paddock.

Ash opened the gate and we stepped through. When I released his head collar, Rebel stood in front of the gate to stop me from leaving. I ducked under his neck and quickly left the yard. He called out as I walked away, reared, and then paced up and down the fence line. He was fretting about me. It was another clear sign that I needed to go to the quack's.

***

In the car, I drifted off to sleep. I couldn't keep my eyes open and had developed a slight wheeze.

When we entered the waiting room, I sat down while Ash filled in a form with my details at the nursing bay. All I wanted to do was lie down, but the chairs were so uncomfortable.

When Ash sat beside me I placed my head on her shoulder and she stroked my hair.

"It's going to be a little while. Do you want me to call anyone?"

"No, they'll just worry and drain what little energy I have at the minute. Keep it to yourself. I didn't let them know I was back for the same reasons. I wanted an opportunity to get settled before I was dragged off to dinners and catch-ups."

"Rest now. I'll wake you when they call your name," said Ash.

I needed no further encouragement. Already in a daze, I fell into a deep slumber as soon as I stopped speaking. My headspace was dark; no dreams occurred. All I experienced was an endless depth of black.

"Talia," whispered Ash as she gently squeezed my hand.

I willed my eyes to open and squinted at the light above my head. I looked around and realised I was in a bed, in a room. I couldn't quite make sense of my surroundings.

"You lost consciousness in the waiting room so you jumped the queue."

In a husky voice, I replied, "Lucky me."

"There's more."

"Hit me with it." I was too tired to really care.

"You started to crash. I thought they were going to have to use the paddles on you. Thankfully you responded to the oxygen mask and regained your O2 stats, and then were rewarded with a room in hospital. They took some X-rays and confirmed you have pneumonia."

"OK, I need to sleep. Go home." I couldn't keep my eyes open and I had a thumping headache.

"Are you sure? I was going to stay here."

"Home, Ash, go home. Please don't tell the others. I'll be fine. I'll call you if I need anything."

She asked again, "Are you sure?"

"Bye-bye now," was all I said before I allowed myself to drift off again.

***

I woke to the sight of a flashlight flicking around in the room. I squinted and shifted slightly in my bed to figure out who it was.

"Sorry I woke you. I'm Patricia, your nurse for tonight. How are you feeling?" she said in a quiet voice.

When I responded, I was surprised at how raspy my voice sounded. "I have a headache and my mouth is really dry."

"Your oxygen intake is low. You need to keep the mask on so we can get you more air. Pneumonia is a very serious problem and your body is fighting hard at the moment." She leant across my torso and lifted my head to place the strap of the mask around it. I didn't have the strength to assist so I lay there like a lifeless rag doll.

"That's it; just keep breathing. I'll make the arrangements to have you prescribed something for your headache and will bring you back a jug of water. Is there anything else you need?"

"Can you switch on the light in the toilet so I know where I'm going, please," I whispered.

"You might want to stick with a bed pan for now. You lost consciousness for quite a while. The last thing you need is to fall over and hurt yourself," she said.

"I'll be fine. Please switch it on."

I fell asleep midway through her taking my blood pressure, jolting awake as she unclasped the cuff. I had never slept so much in my life. My whole body vibrated as I struggled to take deep enough breaths to fill my rigid, crackling lungs. Patricia finalized the rest of her duties and turned on the light before leaving the room.

***

The next time I opened my eyes, Brad was present, holding my hand and staring at me.

"Hey, you," he said with a half-smile. I could see he was worried.

"I guess Ash caved and told you."

"So she bloody should. What were you thinking, hiding this from me?" he said, clearly frustrated.

"I need to sleep. Go home, Brad. I don't have the energy to argue. I'll be fine," I said, removing my hand from his grasp and doing my best to adjust my body to a new position. I was already waging an internal battle; I didn't need an external one.

"No, you need to eat. They said you've been in here for three days and all you've done is sleep. If you don't start eating soon they may threaten to place a tube in your stomach."

I slowly turned my head to show Brad the scowl on my face. "You're making that up."

"No, I'm not," he said, folding his arms. "Do you want me to call a nurse in to tell you?"

"Help me sit up," I said.

Brad leapt to his feet and leant forward. His annoyance seemed to melt away as he realised that I was truly weak and not myself.

"It's OK. Don't move. I'll lift you," he said in a soft tone.

"Thanks," I said when he was finished.

"I'm going to get you something to eat. What do you want?"

"Just some soup and a glass of water. My mouth is really dry."

"OK, I'll be back."

***

When Brad returned, he had a hospital tray filled with items. He shifted the day table over my bed and placed the tray on top. A nurse with a smile that seemed to radiate with too much happiness for a hospital came in. What was worse, she seemed to hold a melody as she spoke.

"How's our patient today?" she asked, checking my temp.

"Ready to go home," I said with my eyes closed.

"Perhaps in a day two but not today, I'm afraid."

I nodded and wondered whether she thought I was serious. I had no strength to stand, let alone go home.

"Can you please draw the curtains? I want them open so I can look out the window."

"Sure," she responded.

"It's OK. I'll get it," said Brad as he leant over, dragging the blinds apart. "Well, I'll be damned."

Lifting my head slightly from my pillow, I asked, "What is it?"

"This tree is full of ravens. I've never seen anything like."

"Move, please. I want to see," I said as I tried to fully open my eyes.

As he stepped aside, the branches of a large tree were revealed and it was indeed jam-packed with ravens. I smiled as they squawked and flapped their wings.

"Yes, they arrived a couple of days ago and we haven't been able to get rid of them," said the nurse.

"They just turned up?" I queried.

"Yes, about three days ago they appeared and have been there ever since. It's the strangest thing. The local rag was looking to do a story on it."

"Talia, do you remember when we were kids lost in the bush. You asked a raven to get us home. You insisted we follow it as it flew from tree to tree. I thought you had lost your mind, but sure enough, it led us back to a familiar path. When you thanked the raven, it squawked and then flew away."

"I remember."

"Perhaps they're here for you," he said in jest.

"Maybe they are. Lucky me," I said, closing my eyes again. I felt comforted knowing they were around. I needed them to watch over me, as I had no strength to do so.

Brad waited until the nurse had finished her assessment before resuming his position on the edge of my bed.

"Open those beautiful brown eyes. Let's start with the soup."

He placed a spoonful of warm soup in my mouth.

I pulled a face as I tried to swallow.

"Are you OK? Does it hurt to eat?"

I lifted my torso forward as I reacted to my gag reflex. "What kind of soup is it? Dirty sock consommé? Fucking yuck."

Brad laughed. "Come on. It can't be that bad." He took a spoonful to try.

As soon as it hit his tongue, I watched the horror on his face as he reefed forward and spat it out. I smiled.

He was like a little boy who had to be burnt to know that fire was truly hot.

"Told you it tasted like arse," I said as a smile landscaped across my face.

At first Brad didn't respond. He just stared at me.

"It's so good to see your smile again," he said in a broken voice.

"Don't stress, Brad. The pneumonia won't kill me but I'm pretty certain this food will. Get it away from me," I said, half-laughing.

"I'll go out and get you a decent meal. Rest. I'll be back."

"Don't hurry," I said as I yawned.

I kept my eyes closed while Brad kissed my forehead and left the room. I really wanted to shower. My hair was plastered to my scalp from sweat and my teeth felt furry. I must look a treat I thought as I drifted off to sleep once more, this time whispering the words *help me heal* as I heard the ravens madly squawking at me.

In the darkness a crystalised voice spoke in my ear, "Welcome, child."

I turned to see a man with yellow eyes and the darkest skin. He was topless, wearing only a pair of torn, navy-blue tracksuit pants and no shoes. On his chest were markings in yellow paint, which I recognised as voodoo symbols. I was about to turn to look around the hut we were now standing in when he sprayed a milky liquid all over my face and body. Instantly, I fell to my knees and lost any sense of myself.

Whacking the top of my head with his large hands, he called out, "Break the fever," over and over.

I felt as though he was drawing out the virus. My body moved back and forth as he continued to grapple with the aliens embedded in my core. A swell rose with force from deep in my lungs to the surface. Sweat poured from me as I started to wail uncontrollably. My body convulsed and my eyes rolled back into my skull, revealing my pulsating brain, and then a surge of fluid projected out of my mouth all over the floor. The intensity of the force made me wish for death, then nothing. I was in a space of blackness again, no pain, no fever, just darkness. It was time to rest.

***

When I woke, my eyes adjusted to see a room filled with people. All eyes were on me. Ruth, Shane, Tommy, Sammy, Brad and Ash.

I attempted to sit up and looked at them while I scratched my itchy scalp. "Hey, guys, how long have you been here?"

Ruth leant forward, throwing her torso over mine, and embraced me. "Talia, we were so worried. You've been in some sort of coma for the last twenty-four hours."

"Coma? No, I was just sleeping. I was tired, but I'm all good now." I smiled and patted her back.

"No, Talia, your pneumonia is worse. You haven't been responding to the medication. It's serious," said Shane.

"Guys, I'm fine. I could run a marathon. Seriously, stop mollycoddling and call in the quack. I need to speak with him."

Ash headed towards the door. "I'll ask the nurse to page him."

"Thanks, big mouth," I said, smiling.

"Come on, Talia, surely you couldn't expect her to keep this a secret?" said Brad, the protector.

I kept my gaze on Ash as I responded, "I guess it was unreasonable for me to trust a person would keep their word." I semi-laughed and then put her out of her misery. "We're cool, Ash, I understand. I'm only teasing."

I could see the relief wash over her. I rubbed my hands together. "That was fun."

"You do look better, Talia," said Sammy.

"She's clearly not sick enough if she's able to hang shit on people," added Tommy.

"I'm fine. I want to go to the toilet, so if you guys don't mind stepping out."

"I'll stay and help you," offered Ruth.

"Nope, all good – everyone out, please."

They left but I could tell they were annoyed with me. I wasn't fussed. My fever had broken, I could breathe again and for the first time in a while my mind was clear. The worst of it was over. As I pulled the sheets back, I realised the buggers had put a catheter in. My first reaction was to rip it out but the last thing I needed was more complications. I opted to wait and started bending my legs instead to get the circulation going again. It took a few attempts at stretching and extending to start to feel connected. I had been in bed for the better part of four, possibly five, days without moving. It was fascinating to see how quickly the muscles seemed to shrink. I guess not eating over that period had contributed somewhat.

The opening of the door interrupted my thoughts. A handsome young man walked in. He possessed an air of confidence, holding his clipboard and stroking his stethoscope.

"Hi, Talia, glad to see you're awake. You had us worried there for a while."

"I guess worry is the theme of the day. Speaking of

worry, should I be concerned that you look like you just graduated from high school?"

A fantastic smile appeared as he shook his head and pretended to look at his clipboard. "Let me see. Ah, yes. Sarcasm is intact. I'll give that a tick, shall I?"

"Nice response. I like it. Hey, Doc, I need to warn you that I'm not superstitious so if you ask me to touch wood, you might be surprised what I reach for. I'm just saying."

I watched as he once again glanced at his clipboard. "Personality clearly intact with a possibly hyperactive flirtatious syndrome."

I laughed. "Sounds serious. Is it curable?"

He raised an eyebrow. "I'm sure when you're fully recovered and back on your feet you will be actively curing said syndrome."

"Are you allowed to say that?" I said, laughing.

"Doctor–patient privilege affords me the luxury."

"I really want this catheter out so I can have a shower. Any chance of doing it now?"

"Hold your horses. Your last X-ray showed the pneumonia had travelled to the lower lobes of your lungs and you went into a coma, so we need to step back for a moment and reassess what we're going to do here."

"All jokes aside, I feel fantastic. I've had more rest during the last few days than I've allowed myself in years. X-ray me and you'll see the infection has cleared."

"Talia, we did the X-ray yesterday when you lost consciousness. There's no way it could clear in such a short time. I know you don't want to accept this, but you're really sick at the moment. We need to find the right medicines to knock it on the head. I'm going to take some sputum samples for the lab. They'll be able to confirm the strain so we can formulate a more definitive plan of attack."

I shifted across so I was now sitting upright with my legs hanging over the edge of the bed. I looked at him with a cheeky expression. "Or we can get an X-ray to prove that I'm right and you can apologise at dinner."

His eyes widened. "Dinner?" he said.

"I'm making a wager between two consenting adults. If I'm correct, you'll take me out to dinner and there will be grovelling added to the menu. If you're right; well, choose your prize." I reached across and grabbed the end of his stethoscope, slowly dragging it from around his neck as I stared into his eyes. "What would you like from me if I lose the bet?"

"It's a silly bet; you will lose, Talia," he said, ignoring my teasing.

In my most sultry voice, I responded, "Well, I guess that makes me a sure thing. What would you like to wager?" I tilted my head, maintaining eye contact as I bit my bottom lip and smiled.

He stared at my lips. "I'll settle for dinner."

"Your words say dinner but your eyes suggest that I'm on the menu." I laughed.

"You're a wicked young lady."

"Right," I jumped up, "let's get X-rayed." I reached for the edge of the bed to regain my balance as I felt my legs give way slightly.

He gripped my elbow. "Take it easy. Seriously, your body's been through the wars. I need you to get better so that you can buy me that well-earned meal. OK?"

I laughed and slowly walked towards the door with my clothesline on wheels displaying my IV bag and catheter outputs beside me. The gang was on the lounge suite waiting to hear what the doctor had to say.

"Hey, we're just going to get an X-ray to check on things. You guys should really head home. Ash, you can stay. I'll need a lift home in a minute."

"Should she really be walking right now? Can we get her a wheelchair?" said Ruth, frowning.

"Ruth, I'm good. If you want to wait, that's fine. I'm not going to argue with you guys. I'll be back in ten."

As we walked down the hall, I paused and turned to look at the doctor. "Do you think my bum looks big in this gown?"

He burst out laughing as we both continued to the X-ray department.

***

When I got back to my room, I looked around for my clothes. The rest of the crew followed me in.

"Talia, you really need to get back into bed," said Brad, who was standing behind me with his hands on my hips.

"Where are my clothes?"

"There, in the wardrobe," responded Ash, pointing behind me.

Ruth and Brad glared at her in disbelief.

"Come on, guys, leave Ash alone. She was only trying to be helpful," I said, laughing. Somehow she always managed to become the piggy-in-the-middle in awkward situations.

I found my things, including my smelly socks and shoes, dumped into a garbage bag. I scrunched my face at the idea of putting them back on.

"Ash, can you take these home and bring me back some clean clothes, please?"

"Sure, Talia," she said as she took the bag.

"She can bring you some clean clothes but you're not leaving. You're sick," said Brad, gently coaxing me towards the bed.

The doctor walked in as I sat on the edge of a stool near the bed.

"What's up, Doc?" I said with a cheeky grin.

His lips were pursed but then he smiled. "Your X-ray is clear. I don't know what you did or how you did it, but there is no sign whatsoever of infection – anywhere."

"Are you sure?" said Ruth, stepping in to look at the X-ray in his hand.

"I'm positive. I've had three other people look at her X-rays from yesterday and the ones we took just now. Her lungs are clear. I can't explain it." He shook his head.

"Guess we can talk about it over dinner tomorrow night. Does 7 pm work for you?"

His face went red. "Sure, that will be fine," he said in a matter-of-fact tone.

"Excellent. The next point of business is getting me detached from all this stuff so I can have a shower. Hopefully Ash will be back by then so I can get dressed and head home."

Brad stepped in. "Don't you think it would be safer to keep her in overnight just to make sure she's OK?"

"Brad, seriously no. I'm going to leave with or without consent, so arguing with me is futile. The X-ray is clear. I feel great. It's time to go home. Give me a chance to settle in tonight and you can all come over and fuss as much as you like tomorrow and I won't resist, promise."

Ruth placed her hand on Brad's arm. "OK, Talia."

"Thank you," I said.

They all left to head home while the doctor remained in the room to detach the IV and catheter. As I lay back on the bed, I watched him work.

"You're making me nervous," he said.

"Is it because I'm watching or because you're secretly a high school kid moonlighting as a doctor and concerned that the jig is up?"

He laughed. "You are an original."

"Indeed. Are we done yet?"

"Patience. I'm almost finished," he said.

"What's your name, anyway?"

"Dr. Rossi. Sorry, I thought I had introduced myself earlier."

"No, we kind of went off on a tangent when you walked in the door. Seriously, after all we've been through together, you haven't volunteered your first name. Wow, perhaps I underestimated the depth of our connection. My apologies. Dinner's off," I said, smiling at him.

He didn't alter his demeanour. "*We* went on a tangent? Mason, my name's Mason."

"Pleased to meet you, Doc. Get my details from the admission form and text my cell where I'm to meet you tomorrow at around 7 pm."

"Will do."

Ash walked into the room.

"Hey, can you put the clothes in the shower room for me? Thanks."

"Sure. Do you need help showering?" she asked.

"I'd say yes, but I think you might get a little handsy in there so I'll take my chances on flying solo," I said, laughing.

Ash laughed too and did her magic trick by going a fluorescent red.

Mason looked at me. "So, you're like this with everyone?"

"Oh, Doc, don't devalue our special moments. Celebrate who I am, not what you would like me to be."

He rolled his eyes. "I'll text you about tomorrow."

"Cool, thanks. Can you let the nurses know I'm going to discharge myself in half an hour or so. I want to do a runner as soon as I'm finished showering."

"Yep, part of my job." He looked at Ash, who was now lying in my bed. "Is she always this bossy?"

"Worse," she said with a hearty laugh.

"Oi, it's uncool to laugh at your own jokes." I went into the shower cubicle, closing the door behind me.

I looked in the mirror and laughed at my reflection. If I had known how precisely horrid I looked, would I have been so cocky with the Doc? Meh, probably. I turned on the taps and waited for the temperature to adjust. The feeling of the water falling onto my skin was the best. My hair soaked up the shampoo, refusing to lather until the third wash and rinse. I felt lighter as the layers of caked sweat and dead skin cells floated down the drain. When I stepped out of the shower and got dressed, I walked back into my room to be greeted by Ash fast asleep on the bed.

"Hey, princess, wake up. It's time to escape from Alcatraz."

Ash stretched her arms out above her head then, quick as a flash, jumped to attention. "Are you ready?" she asked, shaking her arms to rid herself of pins and needles.

"Let's get the fuck out of here," I said, elated at the idea of breathing fresh air.

***

At the nurse's station I was greeted with disapproving eyes. My X-rays were on the light box and a crowd of staff were looking at them.

"Do you need me to sign any discharge papers or can I go?"

The matron leant forward. "We have them ready. Are you sure you want to leave?"

I picked up the pen and looked at the papers she had placed in front of me. "Where do I need to sign?"

She pointed to the sections.

I signed them and then returned the pen. I took one last look at the crowd staring at my X-rays and walked out the door.

The cool afternoon breeze was fantastic. As I walked away, I felt a heightened sense of freedom. "Ash, I just need to take care of something. If you bring the car around, I'll meet you back here."

"Do you want me to come with you?"

"Nope, all good. I'll see you in a minute." I walked around the corner, looking for the tree with the ravens. I could see it near the end of the building. There weren't as many perched on the branch as there had been the day before. Still, there were enough to be impressive. I waved my hands in the air and started to twirl around in circles, saying, "Thank you," over and over. I wanted to ensure they knew I was leaving. The birds squawked and took flight, circling high above my head three times clockwise before commencing their next journey. I was left dizzy and grateful.

***

The next morning while I was out riding Rebel, I received the text from Mason with the details about our meeting. Ruth and Suzanna came over at midday to bring food and to check I was still alive. Brad was nowhere to be seen. I guessed he was still angry with me for not telling him I was unwell. He probably just needed a few days to process how he felt.

When Ruth and Suzanna had left, I thought about my date that night. I decided I would wear a dress to dinner. I rarely got out of my jeans and T-shirt. It was time to make an effort to look and feel feminine. Ash helped me straighten my hair and we even put some nail polish on my hands and feet. The last time I had been this dolled up was at the masked ball. As I jumped in the car and drove down the driveway, I could see Ash in the rearview mirror waving manically and smiling like a fool. *Crazy kid.*

***

The restaurant he had chosen was called the *Solitary Muse*. It was a small country café house during the day and in the evening was converted into a candle-lit Italian-influenced eatery. When I walked in, Mason was already seated. He raised his hand to gesture me through.

"Well hello, Doc," I said as he stood up to acknowledge my arrival.

"Wow, I mean wow. You look amazing."

His hair was slicked back, a portion of his fringe falling forward in a slight kink. He was wearing dark blue jeans and a black loosely fitting shirt.

"You scrub up OK yourself," I said with a cheeky grin.

"I've ordered this shiraz and poured us each a glass. I hope you don't mind."

"Red's good and I love shiraz." I sipped the wine. It was delicious. "Australia definitely has some of the best vineyards in the world."

"Have you travelled much?"

"I've travelled enough for three lifetimes and I'm still yet to see many of the wonders in this world. Let's have a quick look at the menu so we can place an order and proceed to the grovelling portion of the evening, shall we?"

Mason stuck out his tongue and scrunched his face like a little playful boy then picked up the menu to make a selection.

The waitress came to our table. The first thing I noticed was her nose ring. She had her mousy-blonde hair tied back, and it appeared to have interwoven rags and dreadlocks.

"Hi, my name is Jenna. I'll be your waitress for the night. Are you ready to order?"

"Hey, Jenna, I'm Talia and this is Mason."

Mason smiled at her. "Hello."

"Hello, are you ready to order?" she politely repeated.

"Yes, I'll have the bruschetta as a starter and the potato and parsnip soup for my main, with a side of the steamed French beans, please."

Mason looked at me and then told Jenna his choices. "I'll also have the bruschetta and for my main I would like the rib eye medium rare with peppercorn sauce, please."

"OK, I'll put the order in. Is there anything else I can get you?"

"You could sate my curiosity?" I said, looking up at her grey eyes.

She smiled and waited for my question.

"I can detect an accent from time to time. What's your heritage?"

"My parents are from Sweden. I was born there. We migrated to Australia when I was eight. I can't hear the accent but many people have asked the same question so it must exist."

"It's only slight but it exists," I said.

She waved the docket. "I better go place this order."

"No problems, thanks."

Jenna walked off and Mason stared at me, smiling.

"What's the look for?" I asked.

"You have this amazing ability to bypass the informalities and reach people. It's fascinating to watch and scary to experience."

"Scary? Really? Explain it to me. I'm curious."

"When you speak to people you hold eye contact. It's something we all crave but very few do it well. It's unnerving to have you stare into my eyes. I feel like you're reading me."

"What if I was reading you? Is it such a bad thing? To know someone better than they know themselves is often the gift you can return by providing insight into what they cannot or choose not to see." I took another sip of wine, all the while maintaining eye contact.

"Read me," prodded Mason.

"Is this a test?"

"No, my request is genuine. Read me. I'd like to see what you see."

"Are you sure?" I asked, concerned.

"Yep, I'm positive. It's not every day you get a beautiful woman looking beyond the surface of your skin."

I took a deep breath and stared into his hazel eyes. "You're an only child. You lost one of your parents when you were young. You were around ten … no, twelve years of age. Old enough to remember and young enough not to understand why you were being robbed of someone you loved. It's your father. The memory of him in the last months before he passed still haunts you. It's possibly one of the key drivers that led to you to become a doctor.

You're single. You want to be in a relationship and crave the ideals but struggle with your false obligations to be there for your mum. You're scared to take the plunge for her and for you. The irony is your mum is worried that you haven't settled down. She wants you to find love, as she did. It's the only thing she worries about. You are her only child, born from the love of her life. She wants to ensure you find happiness and companionship."

I paused to take another sip of my wine and Jenna came back with our entrees.

"Thanks, Jenna," I said as she placed them on the table.

She smiled and walked away.

Mason continued to stare at me.

"Are you OK? How did I do?" I asked, knowing by his reaction I had hit a home run.

"How did you get all of that from just looking at me? I don't understand how it's possible."

"That's the difference between you and me. You spent your whole life searching to make sense of things, whereas I accepted the truth of what had happened without question or struggle. It was always part of who I was. I looked at the core of you and what I told you was exactly what you wanted me to know."

I looked down at my bruschetta. "We should eat before it gets cold." I picked up my knife and fork and Mason did the same. I was surprised at the quality of the food. Considering we were in the country, I hadn't expected it to be so tasty.

"Yum, who's the chef? This is really delicious," I said.

"The owner's son has returned from a stint overseas, where he did his chef apprenticeship. I believe he's the one who has taken over the night duties. I agree: it tastes really good."

It didn't take long for us to consume our meals.

I leant in and whispered, "Make a distraction. I'm going in to lick the plate."

We both laughed.

"How did you do it?" he blurted.

"Seemingly heal myself overnight?" I responded.

"Yes. It defies explanation and yet you did it. How? I haven't been able to stop looking at your X-rays."

"So what's the verdict, Doc, do I have a nice set of lungs?" I said, amused at my own humour.

"Funny. Now spill the beans. I really need to know."

"The body has an amazing capacity to heal. Do you recall all those ravens in the tree outside my room?"

"Yes, it was bizarre. They're all gone now. I checked this morning while executing my rounds."

"I know. I said goodbye to them and they flew away when I left. You see, when I was a child I was thrust into an esoteric space. It allowed me to cross the boundaries of what is our perceived reality. I was young and knew no different. I grew up feeling its essence surge through me like a life force, a trusted friend."

He leaned forward over the table, resting his chin on his hands. "OK, I'm listening."

"The pneumonia hit me like a sledge hammer. My mind was foggy, my resolve weakened. I consider ravens my guides, so their presence reminded me that sometimes I need to ask for help. I called on the universe to assist me in healing and the universe responded. I crossed planes, which to you appeared as a coma. I worked with a healer to remove the infection embedded in my vessel and post this was transported to a space of nothingness, where my body could start the journey to recovery."

"Is it like a dream state?" he asked, still trying to apply logic.

"No. It's as real as we are to one another right now. If you get cut, you bleed. When you return, you bear the scars of whatever you experienced. The price paid for crossing over is an exchange of energy. You give and receive in equal proportions," I said.

"I'm struggling to understand it. I can't imagine such a space exists."

"How much of what I told you about yourself was accurate?" I asked.

"All of it. You had me pegged right from the start," he said.

"Do you know why I shifted from the suggestion of ten years old to twelve?"

"Hit me with it." He lifted his fists in play.

"It was because your finger tapped the table top twice when I said ten. I knew my two previous statements were accurate because subconsciously you were supporting my direction because you wanted me to see."

"Here you go," said Jenna as she removed the entrée plates and replaced them with our mains.

"Thanks again, Jenna."

"You're welcome," she said in a quiet voice.

I watched her walked away and could feel her essence was consumed by a level of sadness. Jenna felt lost.

"My main looks fabulous. I can't believe you only ordered soup for yours," said Mason, already carving into the side of the beast he had ordered.

"I hadn't eaten in days so I'm not about to gorge on a heavy meal. I'm a light eater at the best of times so this hearty soup will be plenty."

"How long have you been a vegetarian?"

"I'm not sure that I am. I really dislike labels. I just eat what I feel like and it happens to be mostly fruit and veggies. I eat pasta and rice at times, completely dislike dairy, so I do my best to avoid it."

"Why the aversion to classification? What's wrong with being known as something?"

"It's restrictive and places people in easy-to-read boxes wrapped up in a web of conditions and rules. It's not who I am. I don't want to have someone label me and then observe something I do, questioning the very label they chose to assign to me."

"So you have strong views on this then," he said, amused at my rant.

"Maybe." I raised my glass in cheers.

"You're fascinating," said Mason as he carved another piece of flesh.

"The head nurse … what's her name?" I asked.

"Her name's Darlene. Why?"

"If you ask Darlene out, she will say yes. I know you want to and she daydreams that you will one day."

"What makes you so sure I'm interested in Darlene? I'm here having dinner with you, aren't I?" said Mason, feeling exposed.

"Mason, Mason, Mason. Your left eyebrow rose when I asked for her name. Your torso readjusted upright to show you were interested in knowing more. Your pulse quickened when I said she daydreams about you. The reason I mentioned her was because she kept staring at you when I was at her station signing the discharge papers. She had a feeling of longing about her. I wanted to let you know she cared and then realised through your behaviour just now it was mutual. Simple."

"Amazing," he said, scratching his head.

"I guess from an outsiders' perspective it may appear amazing. I'm just able to pay attention to details most overlook. The facades and brick walls people falsely shield themselves with are transparent to me. I see because I devoutly pursue truth and do my utmost to be open to the possibilities."

"Why did you ask me out?"

"I didn't. You lost a bet, remember?"

"You flirted with me from the moment I walked in the door. It was confusing."

"No, it was fun, playful. I apologise if it was confusing. It wasn't my intent. I felt compelled to play with your soul and did, with no more intent than to bring some joy into your space of silent sadness."

"You could tell I was sad?"

"Yes. When you walked in I was overwhelmed with relief at regaining my health, so I shifted your sadness to moments of joy as a way of giving back to the universe."

"Thank you," he said in a soft voice.

"No, thank you, Mason. I don't believe I've ever given any one person this much insight into who I am. It's a testament to your energy. Thanks for wanting to know and for listening even though you don't understand," I said.

"Can I get you anything else?" asked Jenna.

"I'd love a coffee, double-shot long black, please," I said. Jenna prompted Mason. "And for you?"

"I'm fine, thanks. The steak was filling." He patted his stomach.

I placed my napkin on the plate. "Can you let the chef know the food was delicious?"

"Sure, I'll do it now," said Jenna.

Mason poured the last of the wine into our glasses. "Do you have your eye on anyone? A love interest?"

"It's funny. The person I feel the most connected to is a ghost to me. An idea of a person presenting signs of existence, drawing my attention and awakening my desires for connection and yet he eludes me in physical form. I guess that must sound crazy."

"Talia, after what I've seen only knowing you for a minute, nothing is crazy. You make the impossible seem plausible."

I smiled. "Indeed, and yet for everything I'm capable of being, this one thing eludes me. I've spent a lifetime being awarded the role of 'unrequited' to many. It never occurred to me I might end up being the same, perhaps worse, because my unrequited is intangible, a ghost. How's that for a tragic love story?"

"Here's your coffee. This dessert is compliments of the chef as thanks for your positive feedback." Jenna placed a couple of delicate mini chocolate mousses in front of us.

"Lovely. Thanks."

"No problems. Enjoy."

I shifted my dessert next to Mason's. "Have both. I don't eat chocolate."

"Who doesn't eat chocolate? It's not a calorie thing, is it? Try some. It's delicious."

"Chocolate makes me feel like death when I eat it. Sometimes I have the seventy percent-plus dark chocolate, but mostly I avoid it." I finished the last of my wine and shifted to sipping on my coffee.

"Have you ever been tested for allergies and intolerances?"

"Nope, don't need to. My body screams at me when I put fuel in that's not welcome. I tend to know what works and doesn't."

"You should look at getting tested. The results might surprise you," Mason insisted.

I released a big sigh. "Not much in this life surprises me."

***

It felt strange letting Mason pay for dinner but it was part of the bet so I let it slide. Before we left, I gave Jenna my details and asked her to meet me on the farm the next day. She seemed cautious but agreed.

As we headed out the door I noticed the neon sign of the Chinese restaurant flashing across the way. I walked towards it.

"One last stop before we bid one another good night." I signalled for Mason to follow.

We entered the foyer, where the owner's daughter sat at the reception desk, bored out of her mind.

She looked at us with a glazed expression. "Only takeaway now. Eat-in has finished."

"Actually, I was interested in grabbing a couple of fortune cookies."

She gave her parroted response. "One dollar each or a bag of ten for five dollars."

Mason placed two dollars on the counter and smiled. "My shout."

I nodded. "Yep, your shout."

The girl rolled her eyes at our dialogue and pushed the bowl of cookies towards us. "Pick one each."

I pointed at the board behind her. "It shows you the sayings they have. Are you ready?"

"Spoiler alert. Geez, it's hardly worth doing now," he said. "Still, a bushel of money would be nice. Let's go for it."

I snapped mine open, pulled out the message and hid it. "You read yours first."

"*A calm sea will not make a good sailor.* Your turn," he said.

I read the message to myself first and then I whispered the words for Mason to hear, "*Give in to love.*"

"Hold on. That's not one of the sayings on the board," he said, taking a closer look at the three options posted.

"I know. I'm the exception to the rule." I turned and walked out the door.

Mason escorted me to my car. "I had an amazing night and you are an exceptional person."

"I enjoyed tonight too. Thanks for coming out to play," I said as I gave him a cuddle.

I opened my door to hop in and spoke my last words to Mason for the evening. "Take a chance on love, Doc. Ask Darlene out. You have nothing to lose and so much to gain. I promise."

He nodded his head, mouthing the words, "Thank you."

Dream Chaser

The next morning Jenna arrived in a taxi. She was wearing a colourful free-flowing gypsy skirt with a white linen shirt. I greeted her at the door.

"I had no idea you had to catch a cab. I'll reimburse you and give you a lift back into town later."

"It didn't cost much. Thanks, anyway." She peered over my shoulder to see the interior of my house.

"Come in. Have you had breakfast? Would you prefer tea or coffee?" I asked.

"A glass of water would be great."

"OK, take a seat in the lounge. I'll be back soon."

When I returned, Jenna was looking through a magazine on the table. She seemed very comfortable considering I hadn't given any reason for asking her to my home.

"What are your work and travel plans at the moment?" I asked.

"I'm working at the *Solitary Muse* part-time cash-in-hand and I try and get some odd jobs here and there. I want to travel more but I need to save up some money."

"What kind of work do you like to do?"

"I'm not sure. I haven't been sure of much over the last couple of years." She looked down at the magazine again.

"I wanted to offer you a job. I already have someone here full-time working for me. Her name is Ashley. If you're interested, I could have you work here three or four days a week and even offer you accommodation as part of the deal. Ash lives in the stable quarters and you could too. It would help you save some money and assist me by having an extra pair of hands around the place. I'm sure we could even organise to give you a lift and pick you up from the *Muse* on the nights you're working."

Jenna was smiling for the first time since I had met her. "Really? Work here?"

"Well, you'd be out there, but, yeah, working on the farm. Come. I'll introduce you to Ash and show you around. Do you know anything about horses?"

"No, but I'd love to learn," she said.

"Desire is a good start. We can build from there. Ash didn't know much either when she first started."

Jenna and I walked across to the stables, where Ash was pottering. "Hey, I want you to meet Jenna. Jenna this is Ash."

Ash turned to greet us and stumbled over her words as her eyes met Jenna's. I stepped back so Jenna couldn't see me give Ash a look while I mouthed the words, 'You're welcome.'

"Well, don't just stare. Say hello, Ash," I said, laughing.

In true style, Ash's face transformed to a lovely shade of crimson. "I'm sorry. Hi."

"Hi," said Jenna in a shy voice.

"I'm going to head back inside and leave you two to

get acquainted. Ash, show Jenna the accommodation and give her a tour of the place and an idea of the tasks she would need to do. When you're done, Jenna, come in and we can chat some more about whether you're interested in joining the team."

"OK, thanks," said Jenna.

Ash looked at me with a sheepish smile. "Yeah. Thanks, Talia."

"Oh, Ash, you're soooo welcome," I said as I walked away, laughing.

Back in my house, I made myself a cup of coffee and sat in my recliner thinking about the two fortune cookie messages I had received. *Follow your dreams; they know the way* and *Give in to love*. If I followed my dreams it would take me back to Solution Manifestation. I had no idea what 'give in to love' meant. If the right person appeared I would hope I recognised their existence and allowed the natural energy of love to flow between us. I guessed time would tell whether I would ever have the privilege of knowing how it felt to fall in love.

I grabbed my keys and headed out the door. I found Ash giving Jenna a tour of the stable quarters.

"I'm going out for a while. Are you kids OK to hang?"

"We sure are," said Ash in an upbeat tone.

"Do you want me to bring you back a late lunch?"

"No, I have some stuff here. I'll make Jenna something when we're hungry."

I gave Ash a cheeky look. "OK. Catch ya later."

***

I headed over to Brad's. I hadn't heard from him, which was never a good sign. I knew I had to make the first move and the longer I left it the worse it would be. When I arrived, I saw his car in the driveway. As I approached the front door, Brad opened it but he didn't greet me. I walked through, closed it and proceeded to the lounge where Brad was now sitting pretending to read the paper.

"Hey, Grumpy Bum, how are you?" I said in attempt to make light of his annoyance.

"I'm fine," he said, not looking at me.

I walked over and knelt in front of him, moving the paper so he had to look at me. I held a warm smile as I was greeted by his glare. "Don't do this. Please," I said.

He folded his arms and continued to look at me. He was angrier than I had expected.

I placed my arms on his knees and laid my head on top. I attempted my best impersonation of puppy-dog eyes and I pouted my lip and whimpered.

"It's not funny, Talia. You could have died," he said.

I whispered, "I didn't catch pneumonia on purpose."

"You should have told me. I didn't even know you were home. Can you imagine how it felt to find out from Ash you were in hospital fighting for your life?"

"What can I say? I was too busy fighting for my life to be afforded the luxury of thinking beyond the moment. I didn't mean to hurt you. It's not something I planned and you know I can't stand a fuss at the best of times. This was not going to be any different. I needed the space to focus on healing." I squeezed his knee as I saw the tears in his eyes.

"I was so scared. You looked awful and I thought you were going to die. I had never seen you like that before. It was horrible."

"I'd never been like that before. The truth is if it happened again I'm not sure I would have done anything different. You were all draining the little energy I had with your concerns and best intentions. I just needed to conserve energy so I could fight my internal battle. Brad, it wasn't personal," I implored.

"Sure it was, Talia. Ash, practically a stranger in your life, knew, and I didn't."

"Ash only knew because she was there. It was circumstance not a conscious choice."

"I don't care. You told her not to tell me."

"I told her not to tell anyone. Anyone, Brad, not you specifically. Anyone," I said, trying to drive the point home.

"I thought we were more to each other. I feel like I've lost you," he said in a voice that transported me back to the night in the meadow.

"You haven't. I love you. I've always loved you and can never imagine a day when how I feel would change. What do you need me to do to fix how you feel?" I asked, lost in the presence of his pain.

"Promise me, no matter what, you won't ever hide anything like this from me again. I don't care about the others knowing, but I have to trust that you'll tell me."

"I promise," I whispered.

"Pinky-swear thumb-touch," he said, holding out his hand.

I smiled and gave him mine.

"You're pulling out the big guns to seal this pact. We haven't done pinky-swear thumb-touch since I was ten." I laughed.

He cracked a smile. "It's required to instill trust back in the family."

"Well, I'm glad it's instilled."

"You're on probation, but with good behaviour, in time we can reassess the situation."

I smiled, relieved he had come round. I had underestimated how upset he was.

I stood up, reclaiming my hand. "Are we good?"

"We're good," he said with a cheeky smile.

"OK. I've got to head back. Ash is showing a girl called Jenna around. I might hire her if she's happy to do the work."

"Don't you want to stay for lunch?"

"Nah, I ate last night. That should hold me for a few days," I said, knowing it would piss him off.

"Not funny. Make sure you eat. You need to keep your strength up. Got it?"

"Yes, sir." I saluted him.

***

When I returned to the farm, I saw Jenna and Ash having a picnic on the grass. The blanket was laid out and on it were egg-and-lettuce sandwiches, and carrot and celery sticks with dips.

"Ladies, you're having a picnic. How grand."

"Would you like to join us?" Ash shuffled across to make room.

"Nope. What do you think, Jenna? Would you like to come and work here for a while?" I asked.

"I'd love to work and live here, if you're still OK with the idea of me boarding."

"Sure thing. You get the same deal as Ash. I'll set up all the details. Welcome on board. You can both play today and start tomorrow. I've made arrangements for an arborist to trim the limbs off those big gums. You guys will need to start making burn piles of all the refuse so we can get them safely burnt before fire restrictions come in."

"No problems," responded Ash, smiling like a giddy-eyed schoolgirl. I loved it.

I turned to head indoors and called out, "Jenna, nice to see you found your smile." I walked inside before she could respond.

***

I spent the next five days playing catch-up with my emails and making calls for Solution Manifestation. The charity was a hive of activity and had a life of its own. It didn't need me at the helm anymore. The team was solid. They knew their roles and executed them with pride. They believed in what we were trying to achieve. I was so proud of them. The final email I opened was from Michael. He had sent me an electronic invitation to his thirtieth birthday party. I had twelve days before the event. I accepted his invitation and then went online and purchased a one-way ticket back to the US.

***

The evening was still. Sparks from the glowing embers in the burn piles sporadically released into the air, as though dancing towards the clouds. The calm of the fires was haunting. Jenna and Ash had done a power of work during the week to gather all the loose debris for burning. I was impressed with their teamwork.

I went outside, intending to sit beside one of the burn piles. As I approached, I noticed something moving in my peripheral vision. Quietly, I continued towards the fire until I realised it was a blanket. Underneath it, I could see the partial silhouette of Ash shifting Jenna's hair before leaning in to kiss her. I had known they would be attracted to one another; I was just surprised to see Ash had moved in so quickly. Twas a good match. Cupid would be proud, I thought to myself.

***

I fell asleep faster than usual and no thoughts occupied my mind as I drifted into the space of dreams. The words *Give in to love* and *Follow your dreams; they will show you the way* floated past, melting into the background of the scenes playing in my mind's eye. I walked aimlessly through empty streets, never feeling alone. He was watching.

"Where are you?" I whispered.

"Say yes," were the only words uttered.

I continued to wander through the streets of my dreams. It was like a labyrinth unfolding before me, concepts and ideas mottled with random-coloured shapes appearing and shifting. I couldn't make sense of anything.

***

In the morning, the only significant component of the dream I had retained was the concept of saying 'yes'. I didn't know what I was suppose to say yes to but understood it was important. I would have to trust the signs when they appeared.

After breakfast, I went to see Ash.

"Morning, Sunshine. Where's Jenna?"

"Howdy. She's gone into town to get some supplies."

"Cool, so how was fire duty last night?"

Ash paused for a moment with a slight smirk. "It was alright."

"Excellent. I've been meaning to ask about Joe. I haven't seen him since I got back. Did you speak to him about how you felt?"

"Yeah, we broke up."

"Hmm, you don't seem too torn about it. Any particular reason?" I revealed an evil grin.

"Spit it out, come on. I know you know," she said.

In the sweetest tone, I responded, "Whatever do you mean, Ash?"

"Don't play dumb. You knew the minute I saw her I was attracted to her."

"Maybe." I chuckled and sang, "Somebody's in love. Her name is Ashley. Ash and Jenna sitting in a tree, K.I.S.S.I.N.G."

"Whatever. You're such a child," she snapped, and then laughed.

"I saw you stroking her hair and kissing her last night. It was sweet. I left before you ruined the vision with chick-on-chick rug-munching," I said, now cracking myself up.

"Talia, you are so wrong on so many levels."

"Thanks for noticing, Ash. It means the world to me," I said, still laughing.

"You're such a shit-stirrer."

I looked straight into Ash's eyes. "Geez, you could just say thank you and get it over with. Come on, Ash. It's like a Band-Aid. The quicker you rip it off, the less it hurts."

Her face was flaming red. "Whatever."

"So, I can safely assume you weren't into me, given you were like a viper on heat, not hesitating to strike at Jenna's voluptuous southern regions."

I was surprised to see Ash's demeanour change. "No, that's not the reason."

"What do you mean? Are you admitting to having a little crush?" I said teasingly.

"Who wouldn't say yes to you? It's more whether you would say yes back. Regardless, it's not the reason." She smiled.

I tipped my head to one side. "OK, I'm curious, what's the reason?"

"Talia needs a friend, not another person developing romantic feelings for her. I wanted to be your friend. I like being your friend."

I smiled. It was a beautiful, unexpected sentiment. "Don't think for a second this is going to make me stop hanging shit on you," I warned.

Shaking her head, she responded, "I would be disappointed if you did."

"Well, OK, then. Off to work." I headed back to the house, smiling.

Ash was my friend. I was touched. Inside the house, I realised I had been so distracted by the conversation I had forgotten to mention I was leaving again. I needed to get myself organised because I had a sneaking suspicion this trip would be a long one.

***

A couple of days before I was due to head off, I went back for a final health check to obtain clearance to fly. The last thing I needed was a collapsed lung or worse while in transit.

"Thanks for making the time to see me, Doc."

"You know you could just call me Mason. It was you who insisted on knowing my first name, yet you never use it," he said, while warming the stethoscope.

"I wanted you to tell me your name because you chose to leave it out. I saw it as sign, an unspoken barrier. We were two people talking and you chose to hide behind a role. I didn't feel the need to use it. I just wanted you to say it. Besides, it's the Aussie way to shorten everything. Doc's quicker to say than Mason." I laughed.

"I can't imagine who would be a match for you, Talia. You're a handful." He shifted closer so he could listen to my heart.

I followed his instructions, taking deep breaths and then releasing them. I watched him closely as he focused on the examination. He had a nice bedside manner and definite charisma. To me he was a little boy who wanted to be loved but didn't know how to go about it.

"Have you asked Darlene out yet?"

He smiled and continued to check me over: blood pressure, temperature, and finally some blood samples. When he had finished, he wrote some details on his clipboard and then lifted his head to greet my stare. "Yes."

"Patient–doctor privileges afford the need for details. When did you ask her out? How did you approach it? Have you had the date or is it pending? Spill it, Doc."

Mason leant back against the desk and folded his arms with a mischievous smile. "I think I prefer the idea of keeping you in suspense."

"Ah, if only you could. You're busting to tell me. I can see the little schoolboy excitement in your behaviour. I believe it's you who would be suffering. I can see things without being told, remember?"

He tossed his head back and released a big hearty laugh. "I asked her out the next day. I couldn't sleep. Your words were replaying in my head over and over. I knew I had to do something about it or be haunted by your words forever more."

"Nice to see I had an influence, Doc."

"Yes, we can call it influence or meddling. Anyway, the next day I asked her out to lunch and she accepted. We spent the hour skipping on the surface of topics, simple banter and then I saw a sign. She was playing with the rim of her coffee cup, her cheeks had flushed red and she was biting her lower lip. I felt a surge of confidence and started to tell her how I felt. At first I fumbled and then I couldn't stop. All my emotions pushed my words out of my mouth like a current's draw on a tide."

I clapped my hands. It was so nice to hear he had made the effort. "Well done, you. How amazing does it feel?"

"Oh, Talia, it's wonderful. She told me she had feelings for me too. I thought my heart was going to explode. I couldn't wipe the foolish smile off my face as we stared at each other. Just before we reached work again, I grabbed her and kissed her. I didn't know I had it in me, but I'm sure as hell glad that I took a chance. I'm so happy."

I walked across and hugged him. I felt him exude joy; he was allowing the wonders of love to be in his life. I could accept not being in the presence of love. However, knowing it exists and denying yourself is sacrilege. Love and be loved was one of my most sacred beliefs. If I were ever blessed with the opportunity, I would hold on with both hands and never let go. I knew this to be true; I just struggled to believe such a person existed for me.

"I'm so happy for you. Just make sure you're always true to how you feel. Honour this and you will create the best foundation for a lasting relationship. I see too many people try to be what they believe the other needs, losing their sense of self along the way. Get swept up in the romance and joy, for sure, just keep true and you will both be ensured you're falling in love with who you really are. Got it?"

"Yeah, I do. It's funny. I think my failing point in my previous relationships was my willingness to compromise because I had an overwhelming desire to please them. Then the reality of being a doctor set in. They would crack the shits because of my hours and I would feel torn. Darlene understands the environment because she's part of it. Kind of perfect, really."

"All is as it should be. Tell me, what's the verdict on my health? Am I clear to fly?" I asked.

"You're fit as a fiddle. I'll call you in the next few days with the blood results. Other than that, you're good to go."

"Thanks. I'll chat to you in the next few days then. Make sure it's nothing but good news!"

He laughed. "Will do."

***

I did the rounds visiting everyone to say goodbye. Ruth wanted to use my departure as an excuse for another family dinner, but I declined. There was too much for me to do. Instead I went to their houses, had a cuppa and a quick chat so they felt the love and I in turn reclaimed some time. I wanted to ensure Ash and Jenna had everything they needed before I left, so we went over all the tasks, worked through the finances and organised the list of people they would need to engage for the horses.

I didn't pack much to take with me. Anything I needed was already in the States so I only took my camera gear, laptop, phone and not much else. I opted to catch a train into town and then a cab to the airport. It suited me to have the time to think. There was a change in the air; I could feel the essence of uncertainty washing over my core. I felt a depth of desire for companionship rising in me and struggled with the ability to see whether it was possible for me to ever find the one who was seeking me.

The flight across was smooth. The attendants seemed genuinely concerned when I declined the offer of any food or beverages. I had water and I never slept on transport, so watching a movie marathon was status quo for me. At the fifth offer from an attendant, I asked her to let the others know not to bother. I had everything I needed.

She politely smiled and asked, "Do you ever say yes?"

I looked at her for a moment, partly surprised at her question, then responded with, "I don't know." My attempt at a little humour.

She smiled and left me to continue watching the movies.

***

When we landed, I went through the queues at customs and then headed for home. It was nice to be back in my apartment. I kept the place uncluttered by design. The walls were white; the furniture was mainly modern, modular in design. In the main rooms, the only colours were derived from the artwork I had purchased on my travels.

In the afternoon I headed into the office to say hello to the gang. I felt blessed as I witnessed their faces light up when they realised I had returned. Solution Manifestation had been born from a desire to give back to the world and in return I had found another level of family. They were more than just employees to me. I appreciated their devotion and belief in the cause and had always been moved by their respect and care for me.

"G'day, I'm back in time for someone's birthday celebrations. Turning thirty is a rather auspicious occasion."

Michael gave me a big cuddle. "I'm so glad you're home. We missed you."

I looked into his eyes. "Thanks for the invite. I'm glad to be back."

I walked around to each of the desks to say a personal hello to the guys before settling into my office. No sooner had I sat down than Blake walked in.

"Stand up and give me a hug," he said with a wonderful bright smile.

He placed me in his arms and swung me around, making a 'grrr' sound. I laughed.

"Looks like my absence was noted. Here I was thinking I didn't count."

"You count; you always count to all of us. Especially me," he said.

"Thanks, Blake. So, any key items you need me to be aware of?"

"No, everything is running smoothly. The donations are continuing to flow in. The projects are running seamlessly. More plans are underway. It's fantastic," he said, smiling.

"Awesome. Maybe we should look at revisiting some of the original ideas that were born out of the three-day seminar. Perhaps it's time to consider which other options could be pursued. It might even be worth looking at creating another three-day session with a themed ball. It was well received the first time. Thoughts?"

Blake rubbed his hands together. "It sounds like a fantastic idea."

"Did you manage to organise the surprise for Michael's party tomorrow night?"

"I sure did. I got the tickets to see the band. It wasn't easy. I had to ring around and pull a few favours because they had been sold out for months."

"Thanks, Blake. Michael mentioned a while ago he loved this band and couldn't get tickets. I know he'll be stoked. It's a good gift."

"No problems. Is there anything else you need?"

"No, I'm good. I haven't slept yet so I might head back to mine and get the whole jet-lag saga over with before I'm dragged out on the town with these young whipper-snappers tomorrow," I said, mid-yawn.

"Good idea. You look a little pale."

"Yeah, I've been a bit run down of late but I'm on the mend."

I grabbed my bag and headed out the door. On my way home, I stopped off at the local fruit and veggie shop to buy some supplies and then headed home for a well-earned rest. I woke up several times in the evening with night sweats. I couldn't recall my dreams but knew I had been dreaming. My jaw was clenched and I felt exhausted from what seemed to be a fight. My lungs may have been clear but I was still physically recovering from my bout of pneumonia. The long flight wouldn't have helped.

***

The next day I woke just after midday. I felt better than I had in a while. I made myself a juice for sustenance and decided to go for a run along the lake.

When I returned, my hairdresser was waiting in the foyer. I had forgotten I had made the appointment.

"Sorry, Maxine, I went for a run and lost track of time. Have you been waiting long?"

She stood up and gathered her things. "No, I only arrived a couple of minutes ago."

"Great, let's go get this over with." I never really liked getting my hair or nails done. I found it cumbersome and boring to have to sit through the process. If I could leave my scalp at a salon and return when it was done I would.

"You make it sound like a chore," she said, knowing very well it was for me.

"You can set up in the kitchen. I'm going to have a quick shower."

***

When I returned, she was already mixing the colour. I had decided I wanted to get some foils to brighten the blonde and contrast my hair underneath with a deep chocolate mocha. It was going to take hours, so I set up my laptop and focused on work.

The end result looked really good. Maxine cleaned up my frayed ends and blow-dried my hair straight. Even I was willing to take a second look at myself in the mirror.

"Max, do you do make-up, by any chance?"

"Of course. Would you like me to do yours now?"

"If you have time, I would appreciate it. I have a thirtieth to go to tonight. I might as well make an effort. I'll fetch my make-up."

"Do you know what you're wearing? If you do show me, I'll match your make-up to the outfit."

"Nah, I haven't rummaged through my wardrobe yet. Just make my eyes pop. That will do."

"One set of popping eyes coming up," she said cheerfully.

***

I kept my eyes closed while she weaved her magic. I was the reluctant canvas who tried to think of other things while she plucked, plastered and smudged.

When she had finished, Maxine stood back to appraise her work. "Your eyes are stunning. Go have a look."

I went into the bathroom and peered into the mirror. I didn't usually like too much make-up; however, I had to agree with Maxine: my eyes looked smoking hot. All I needed was a touch of lip gloss and I would be good to go for the evening.

I handed over the money. "Maxine, you outdid yourself. I love the way my eyes look. Thanks for swinging past."

"You're welcome. Call me when you're ready for the next appointment."

"Will do. Just shut the door behind you."

"OK. Thanks, Talia."

I went into my bedroom to raid my closet. It had been so long since I had worn anything other than jeans and T-shirts I had no idea if I had anything suitable to wear. I rummaged through the drawers and then went back to the hanging space. I found a pair of dark-blue denim jeans and a white top. The neckline plunged to a lace tie-up. Mostly I liked the sleeves, as they had large open lace embroidery on the bottom quarter of the sleeve. It was understated and feminine. So jeans and fancy T-shirt it would be.

***

I met the guys at *Seeds*, a new hip restaurant quickly becoming famous for growing a large amount of the food they served on a plot at the back and above their premises. The whole team and a few of Michael's friends were present. I was, of course, fashionably late.

I snuck around so I was behind Michael. I leant in, giving him a kiss on the cheek. "Happy birthday."

He turned his head to look at me. "Thanks, Talia, and can I just say 'wow'."

"Yes, yes, you can. I believe you just did," I said, smirking at his reaction.

The food didn't disappoint. The broad-bean salad was out of this world. They made such a simple dish not only look like food porn, it had a taste explosion when you ate it. I was definitely a fan. At the end of the meal I fixed up the tab while Blake announced the surprise access to watch the *Jesters* at the *Lake House Lounge*.

I could hear Michael screaming like a girl.

When I returned, he leapt on me. "Thank you, thank you, thank you."

"Happy birthday, Michael. Please detach," I said in jest.

"You're going to love them, I promise. Let's go. I'm so excited." He jumped up and down.

"You guys go ahead. I'm going to call it a night," I said, hoping I could get away.

"No way. You're not leaving. You never come out with us. Please come. Say yes," pleaded Michael.

"If you drop your high-pitched squeal a notch, maybe," I said, laughing.

"Yippee!" He bounced up and down.

I waved my hands in the air. "OK, everyone take note: no more drinks for Michael."

They all laughed as we headed out of *Seeds*. People walked in droves towards *Lake House*, which was located three blocks east of where we were. My phone buzzed. It was a message from Mason, asking me to call.

"Guys, I need to make a phone call. I'll meet you there in ten minutes. Stick near the bar so I can find you."

Blake walked over. "Do you want me to wait with you?"

"No thanks, I'll be fine. As soon as I've finished this call, I'll head over."

"OK, see you in a minute. If you're not there in twenty, I'm coming to look for you," he warned.

I smiled and waved him to go as I looked up Mason's cell and dialled.

"Hey, Talia, thanks for getting back to me."

"No probs. Is everything all right?"

"You're really low on vitamin D. Most people are as a rule but yours is really low. You need to get a supplement from a health food store and try getting some time in the sun over the next couple of weeks. You don't need to overdo it. If it's not too hot, try ten to fifteen minutes a day. OK?"

"Is that it? Anything else in the results I should know about?"

"No, all the rest of the results are fine. How did you cope with the flight?"

"I had more jet-lag than usual. I broke out into a fever in my sleep last night but felt far better than I have since I got sick, so I guess it's a good sign."

"Just be careful. Don't overdo it. You may have recovered quickly but it doesn't exclude you from a relapse. Lots of sleep, no stress and eat well."

"Sound advice, Doc. I might even listen to it."

"OK, I have to run. I've got to get organised for rounds. Thanks for everything, Talia."

"You're welcome, Mason."

I felt relieved to know I had no major health concerns. The vitamin D was easy to resolve and I needed to make more time for exercise. It had been forever since I had trained in martial arts. I missed the feeling of pushing past the pain threshold into a zone I could only describe as meditational. The pneumonia had hit me hard and fast. It had attacked my body and numbed my mind, a harsh reminder of human fragility.

When I walked into the bar, I could hear the band. It surprised me when I realised they were Irish rock. As they came into my view, I stopped to look at them on stage. It was a small venue with a reasonably large crowd all immersed in the energy of the music. I was caught off guard when I realised the singer was now staring at me and pointing. I shook my head and smiled before walking over to the bar to find the others.

"Talia, over here," called Michael, who was bopping to the music.

"What are you drinking?" asked Blake.

"Vodka, neat. Thanks."

Blake leaned across the bar to yell the order to the bartender. "One vodka neat and a bourbon and coke, please."

When I turned to watch my drink being poured, I noticed the label on the vodka bottle said *yes*. I smiled. It seemed this was a theme in my life at the moment. The word 'yes' appeared everywhere. Say yes. Yes to what? I wondered.

We listened to the band play a couple more songs. I could have sworn the singer was looking straight at me. There were so many people in the crowd I couldn't imagine why he would be fixated on me.

"Talia, I think Eddie the singer has a thing for you. He keeps staring over here. It's you he's looking at," screamed Michael in a high-pitched voice.

I turned to face the bar, my back to the band. "Don't be ridiculous and keep your voice down."

The music stopped and a voice with a lyrical Irish accent spoke. "An angel has turned her back on me."

I ignored the words and continued to sip on my vodka, cringing because he was clearly referring to me. If I could have found a quick exit through the crowds, I would have gladly done so. The attention was not what I desired, not tonight.

"Guess I need to go to the angel if she won't come to me," he said.

Michael tapped on my shoulder. "He's coming, he's coming."

The crowd noise rose as he passed through the sea of people to make his way to the back of the pub where I was standing.

"Michael, judging by the way you're carrying on, I might say the same about you. Take a chill pill. I don't want a fuss," I said, starting to feel trapped.

I turned to face the stage again, knowing by the energy shift in the crowd that he had almost reached me. I casually sipped on my drink when he arrived and stood directly in front of me. The crowd was manic and Michael joined their clamour to touch him.

"You are an angel. I couldn't keep my eyes off you," he said, looking directly into my eyes.

Not knowing what to say, I simply responded with, "Thanks."

There was a glint in his eye as he swung around and announced to the crowd he couldn't play another set until he had my number.

They all started to chant, "Say yes, say yes," over and over.

He turned back to face me. "Take a chance; say yes. Who knows? Lightning might strike."

The bartender tapped me on the shoulder to pass a felt-tipped pen to me. Michael and even Blake were screaming along with the crowd. I took the pen, rolled up the left sleeve on his arm and wrote Talia Jacobs and my cell number. He leant in and politely kissed me on the cheek before he turned to the crowd, raising his arm in triumph. As he climbed back on the stage, he asked to borrow a phone from someone in the crowd. I saw an arm rise up, passing him a cell. I laughed as my phone vibrated. I pulled it out of my pocket, waving it in the air so he could see it was my number. The crowd went into hyper-mode for the next set they played. Michael was beside himself about touching his idol. All I wanted to do was crawl under a rock.

"OK, guys, I'm heading home. I've had enough excitement for one night."

"I'll walk you out, Talia. I'm going to head off too," said Blake.

As we navigated through the crowd, I found everyone was eyeballing me. They all wanted it to happen to them. What they didn't realise was that I would have preferred that it had been one of them and not me. I had no need for attention. I only wanted to find my truest love; it was the only thing that mattered to me now. I wanted to find him without distraction.

"I'm impressed with your ability to draw men like moths to a flame," said Blake, smiling.

"Yeah, me," I said in a sombre tone.

"You're strange. Most people would kill to have something like that happen to them. You seem almost disappointed. Why?"

"I don't want them all, Blake. I just want one, the right one for me. The yin to my yang," I said as I looked up at the expanse of the night sky.

"I'm not sure what 'yin to my yang' means, but if you want it you'll find it."

"I'm not sure he exists," I whispered.

Blake stepped in, placing his arms around me. "He exists. You just need to believe he exists, because he does."

I could feel myself getting emotional. I didn't want to cry. "Thank you," I whispered into his shoulder.

***

My dreams that night were a mottled fusion of the evening's events. The chant of the people in the crowd screaming 'say yes', the words 'lightning could strike' and my mobile lighting up as he called my number were the most prominent imagery. I was so tired of the cryptic messages supplied by the universe. It seemed as though I was always expected to identify the signs and decipher the riddle. Whatever my dreams were trying to convey, I didn't have the energy to play 'solve the puzzle' today. I could feel myself loosing faith.

***

In the office the next day, Michael was bright as a button, clearly invigorated by the night of celebrations. The rest of the team also seemed exceptionally bubbly.

"OK, guys, you have ten minutes to get it out of your system and then you need to put it to bed. Shoot. Ask away."

"How did it feel to have that happen?" asked Georgina, my receptionist.

"Not fun, Georgie. I appreciated his grand gesture and the romance behind his reaching out, but I'm not the one for him so it holds little value for me. Next?"

Michael blurted, "Are you going to catch up with him? You have to go on a date with him."

"'Have to' is not in my vocab. I don't have to do anything. If he calls I will honour the extension and meet with him, but I won't be waiting by the phone."

I was surprised at how many questions continued to be asked. It highlighted how they all wanted to believe in fairytales. Starved of ideals they lacked in their own existence, they idolised being witness to a fantastical story. I didn't believe in fairytales.

As I entered my office, I saw a large package wrapped as a gift on my desk. I hesitated as I heard everyone following me to my door. I turned to see them all looking at me like naughty children.

"What's up?" I said, smiling at them.

"It's a 'welcome home' gift from us. Open it," said Michael, gesturing me forward.

I ripped off the paper to reveal a large picture frame displaying a collage of letters. I looked at them and then back at the team.

"Who are these from?"

"It's our selection of some of the best love letters written to you by strangers wanting to meet you. We sent everyone the standard response, as you asked, but thought you needed to have a snapshot of the best to show you the effect you have on people. The effect you have on us," said Michael as the others nodded to conquer.

"Wow, thank you. This is a really nice gift. I appreciate the thought, guys."

The team went back to work while I sat at my desk, propping up the frame so I could read some of the letters. The depth of the words moved me. These letters held so much heartache and desire to find their truest love. I felt as though I wasn't alone. I may not have been able to meet their needs, but I could understand their desires. I was inspired to write back to these gentlemen. They deserved more than a standard response to their letters. It was the least I could do.

The words poured out of me as I wrote response after response. Some of their sentiments drove me to tears. I wasn't sure if I was crying for them or aching for me. I found myself whispering the words, *Find me. I'm ready. Find me.* My phone startled me as a text message came through.

I got your number last night; meet me for coffee at Launder Coffee House say 2pm? Let me know if you need the address.

I looked at the text and was reminded of the words Mr. Irish had said, 'Take a chance: say yes. Who knows? Lightning might strike.' I decided to go with the flow.

I was feeling disheartened, perhaps even a little lost. I almost wished I had never admitted my truest feelings to myself. Life was easier without desire for what appeared to be unattainable.

I replied: *I know the place. See you at 2 pm.*

I left the office slightly earlier so I could walk to the coffee house. It gave me a chance to clear my mind. I wasn't nervous about catching up with Mr. Irish. I felt as though I was going through the motions to see where it led, not because I believed it would amount to anything. When I walked in, he wasn't there. I was slightly early so I sat on a bar stool facing the streetscape, flipping the pages of a trashy magazine.

"Hi, Talia."

I turned and stood up to look at the man addressing me. "Hi, do I know you?" I asked, looking around the coffee shop for Mr. Irish.

"Daniel, the lead singer in the band last night, used my phone to call, which is how I got your number," he said.

I looked into his eyes and felt a familiarity about his presence. "Why do I feel like this isn't the first time we've met?"

A wry smile landscaped across his beautiful face. "We have met before. You held a masked ball and I had the honour of dancing with you. My name is Billy."

I reached across to accept his handshake. As we touched, I felt an electric pulse of energy exchange. I looked down at our hands clasped together.

"You felt that too, didn't you?" he said, almost relieved.

I released my hand and ignored his question. "Billy, the man with nice eyes whose smile held secrets. I recall dancing with you."

"I must have made impression for you to remember me after one dance," he said, looking smug.

"Sure, or you could consider I have an exceptional memory for most details. Still, there's something you're withholding. What is it?"

He smiled as he reached into his pocket to retrieve something. "Hold out your hands and close your eyes."

I raised an eyebrow and laughed. "Really?"

"Trust me, Talia. Close your eyes."

We were in a public place. I figured it was safe so did as he requested.

"Hold your hands out."

As I lifted my hands and held them out I heard him step forward into my personal space. I felt his breath on my left ear as he whispered, "A little boy always keeps his promise."

Tears moistened my eyes as he placed something in my hands. When I opened them there was the plait Marlee had created for us when we were kids. I stared at it and unashamedly released the tears to show how moved I was by this moment. When I looked up, he was crying too.

In a broken voice, he said, "Bodhi. You knew me as Bodhi."

I felt an overwhelming surge of emotions which drew me into his arms. We embraced as we cried, holding one another tighter than two strangers ought to.

I closed my eyes and whispered, "What the fuck took you so long?"